MODEL FOR MURDER

MODEL FOR MURDER

STEPHEN MARLOWE

WILDSIDE PRESS

Published by Wildside Press LLC.
www.wildsidebooks.com

CHAPTER ONE

First I opened the door. Then I shut it. Then I opened it again. The bellhop scratched half-heartedly at a pimple the stiff collar of his uniform had irritated, and stared at me. I stared back and shut the door in his face and opened it.

"Honest, the lock works," he said.

"The snap lock." I pointed out. I twisted the key on my side of the door, watching the latch click easily into place and then out. The bellhop snickered and walked past me into the room with a quart of gin, a fifth of vermouth, a bucket of ice and two cocktail glasses on a circular red tray. He dropped his burden on the scarred top of the dresser, adding to the damage. He held out his hand and waited while I was trying to decide which looked better, the tray of gin, vermouth, ice and cocktail glasses or the mirrored reflection of the tray of gin, vermouth, ice and cocktail glasses.

"Thank you, sport," he said, as I gave him a quarter. It had been so long since I'd handed out gratuities I didn't know if he was kidding or not. After he left, I decided to wait for Jo-Anne before I unfastened the cap on the bottle of gin, so I stretched out on the bed, laced my fingers behind my head, stared up at the cracked ceiling and tried to savor the feeling of freedom. Which was easy.

Take the lock. I could open it and shut it, as often as I liked or not at all. I could play the radio at three a.m. or dance a jig up Park Avenue and watch the dog-walkers or wait for Jo-Anne to drink martinis with me or write my congressman.

Or, I could do nothing. Just plain nothing. I could lie here on a cheap hotel bed which had begun to get the gunwale sag, like so, and take off my shoe to poke indelicately at the blister on my left heel. They were new shoes and maybe I'd complain and maybe I wouldn't, but it was up to me.

This sure beats prison, I thought, wondering if there were any awards for the understatement of the year.

Maybe I'd visit my brother Ken tomorrow and maybe I wouldn't. Whatever I felt like. But I took Ken's check out of my pocket and looked at it again. The little slip of pink paper was undeniably fascinating.

Pay to the order of JASON CHASE—*One hundred thousand and* 00/100 *dollars*. Ken had signed his bold, blocky signature with a broad pen. *KENNETH LAMAR CHASE.*

The check was good. Ken could probably write four or five more like it. It was too damned good and I wanted to tear it up. Instead, I jammed it back in my pocket and told myself I was doing that because I wanted to tear it into little pieces in front of Ken's face and watch his expression, but I knew it was because I still hadn't made up my mind about that hundred thousand dollars.

Then there came a knock on the door and I padded barefoot across someone's faded idea of a floral pattern, to let in Jo-Anne.

Everything Jo-Anne does is enthusiastic, even the way she breathes. I was willing to bet she would go so far as to die enthusiastically, say in sixty years or so. She could cry as enthusiastically as she could laugh, and probably get just as much of a charge out of it. All this being the case, I wasn't exactly gloomy about spending my first evening of freedom with her.

Jo-Anne walked into the room. Expressively. Her first step said it was a pretty shoddy room but she'd been in far worse and anyway, it had a certain charm. Her second step said she was glad to see me. Her third step brought us in contact and her fourth step served as a fuse.

She was kissing me. I was kissing her. I'd been wondering what it would be like to hold a woman after two years. Now I knew.

"Jason," she babbled against my ear. "Let me look at you." That way, it was impossible. "Let me touch you." She already was. "I think it's just wonderful. I think it's the most wonderful thing in the world."

The first thing I did was take those harlequin glasses from her nose and deposit them on the bed. Her eyes were gray as fog at dusk, but flecked with green. Her hair was short-bobbed, fluffy chestnut. She wore a blue plastic raincoat which made crinkling noises between us. She was twenty-six but looked and sometimes acted ten years younger. She had an IQ around 160. Drop Einstein's brain in a dancer's pixie body and you'd come close.

By the time I got the pitcher down from the glass shelf over the sink in one corner of the room and began plinking ice cubes in it, Jo-Anne had removed the raincoat. The way she was dressed told me she thought it was an occasion, my coming out of jail, and on St. Valentine's Day at that. Except that Jo-Anne was not my valentine and knew it.

"Like?" she said, and spun for me to see.

It was a copper-colored dress looking like a coat of copper paint sprayed on the pale shoulders and ridged over the jutting breasts and tucked against the flat waist and flared on the round hips and sheathed across the long firm thighs. "Like," I said, uncapping the gin bottle and sloshing half the contents into the pitcher of ice.

Jo-Anne came over and trickled some vermouth after it and, minus the olives, we were in business. I poured the cocktail glasses full.

"To how you feel about the first gal you saw since getting out," said Jo-Anne, raising her glass. "I hope it's me."

"The first I saw real good."

"What a chance for Jo-Anne Stedman," Jo-Anne said. "You wouldn't kid a girl."

"I didn't invite anyone else, Jo. You."

"Jase, listen. I wanted to visit you up there. Three times I started out but changed my mind. I didn't want to see you like that, in a striped suit or whatever they wear. I didn't want you to see me through a grill fence so we could only touch fingertips." She tilted her glass and I watched the smooth throat work as the martini went down. I poured again for both of us and spilled the rest of the gin into the pitcher.

"Let's just forget about it," I said.

"All of it?"

"What the hell, Jo. I can try. You know why I invited you here?"

"Don't say it."

"I—"

"Please, Jase. Saying it only makes things lousy."

"No. I mean it's different now. I only want to talk."

"I'll bet." Jo-Anne winked at me. The martini had begun to work on the whites of her eyes. Outside, you could hear the steady cold rain hissing on the roof. I walked to the window and rolled the yellowing shade up far enough to rub a circle of windowpane clear of mist and watch the rain swamping the street lamps four floors below and the red tail-lights of cars crawling north on Eighth Avenue.

"What are you thinking, Jase?" Jo-Anne's hands, tangible but almost weightless, were on my neck, the fingertips marching back and forth. She smelled of perfumed soap and martinis. "Are you thinking of Julia?"

I turned away from the window and bumped against her. "To hell with Julia. To hell with all of them. Julia and her old man and my brother." I explored in my pocket and found Ken's check, unfolding it under Jo-Anne's nose. "To hell with this, too."

Maybe I would really have ripped it, but Jo-Anne's fingers wrapped around my wrists and she said, "My God, Jase. A hundred thousand. Is it good?"

"Good and dirty," I said.

"Is it because he married your girl?"

"Nope. Because I took his two-year vacation for him. Julia wasn't in the bargain."

"You said to hell with them." Jo-Anne poured this time and we toasted. "To hell with them." We drank. Then she reached for me. "Put the check away, Jason Chase."

Those first kisses with the crinkling raincoat between us and Jo-Anne's hair all wet were just to say hello, but now she tilted her head and I could feel her lips parting under mine and her heart pounding against my chest and the long smooth roundness of her trembling a little as she got her hands behind my back and squeezed. I barely managed to pocket the check. Every time I wanted to pull away and tell her it was going to be different now, altogether different, she yanked my head back down over hers. Her lips tasted like martinis and honey and she had always been second fiddle to Julia and now seemed willing to be second fiddle to a torch, and I knew the hundred thousand dollars had nothing to do with it.

"That's all right," Jo-Anne finally said. "That's delicious. We'll have to send you to jail more often."

"They sent me, all right. They played me for every kind of sucker in the book."

"Just let me stick around. You'll get over it. Please, Jase. Don't send me away."

"Hey. You're crying."

Tears were in her eyes and on her cheeks. We sat together, on the edge of the bed. I looked down at the floor, at the faded floral pattern, then at her brown suede pumps, her nyloned legs, her copper-paint dress. The rain was still hissing outside, far away like steam. Her hands found nothing to grab on my brush-cut hair, but she clasped them behind my head, leaning forward from the waist. She was warm and had that perfumed-soap smell where her breasts swelled apart.

"I can be good for you, Jase," she said. "Really I can."

"I won't send you away," I told her.

* * * *

It was cold in the room when I awoke. Jo-Anne had turned on the bed lamp and I saw her clothing folded neatly across the back of a chair. I couldn't tell if it was still raining because the shower was going in the bathroom.

I sat up when the bathroom door opened and Jo-Anne emerged in a pale billowing cloud of steam.

"Hi," she said, and smiled. "It's almost three o'clock." She was all white curves and shadows in the dim light, with the same long legs I remembered years ago. "I don't mind," she said. "You can keep on looking if you want. It's almost like we're married if you look. If you stop, you'll embarrass me."

I said nothing and watched her dress, thinking all the time I shouldn't have taken her like this, not tonight, not loving her here in this room while thinking of Ken and Ken's wife, Julia, probably in bed together a few blocks to the east on Park Avenue where a man can live well if his brother spends two years in jail for him. But it had always been like that between Jo-Anne and me, not waxing, not waning, but a steady flame which was too bright in some ways and not enough in others. And maybe it would have been better, I thought, if I'd found a woman who wanted money and no questions and no answers and would have been gone out there somewhere in the rain when I woke up.

"You don't owe me a thing," Jo-Anne said. "Nothing at all, Jase. I wanted to just as much as you did, don't forget that. I never stopped loving you. Will you see me again?"

"What kind of a heel do you think I am?"

"That's what I mean. Owing me something. You can be a heel, if you want."

"I want to keep on seeing you, Jo. Whenever I can. Whenever you're not too busy with that social work of yours."

"Social work? Me? Brother, you've been away a long time! We're all climbing on the Kinsey bandwagon, didn't you know?" She laughed. "Remember Dr. Kincaid up at school?"

"Tall skinny guy? The one who used to say—I quote—we're all going to hell via the highway of moral and ethical debauchery?"

"You've got him. Well, he's working on a book called *Twentieth Century Morality*, and I'm on the staff. Brother, we out-Kinsey Kinsey!"

"Meaning what?"

"If you're really interested, I can show you. Come on."

I grinned at her. "It's almost three o'clock in the morning."

Jo-Anne slipped the copper dress over her head, smoothing it into place with long, graceful motions of her hands. "Zip me," she said and turned around while I went to work on the back of the dress. "Of course, you'll have to keep it secret. Promise?"

"Sounds like one of those gags of yours," I said unhappily. That had been her big weakness all through school. Jo-Anne was a compulsive practical joker.

"Correct. I'm the perennial hotfoot gal, remember? Old funny-girl Stedman—and Dr. Kincaid's so sober and grim about his findings, anyway, I just had to do it."

I climbed into my clothing quickly. "You just had to do what?"

"Borrow Doc Kincaid's research papers and pretend they were stolen. They're over at my place right now. Phyllis is probably sleeping on them, if I know Phyllis."

"She's a joker too?"

"Phyllis Kirk happens to be my roommate. Nice gal if you like them small and plump, with dimples."

"I like them like you," I said, and stood up to kiss Jo-Anne lightly on the lips. "Now, what did you borrow?"

"Dr. Kincaid's questionnaires. They're in code, of course, but according to Doc, half of New York City could be blackmailed with the information they contain. Could be, too. What kind of kiss was that?"

We both enjoyed it better on the second try. "Sleepy?"

"No. But don't get any ideas. We'll take the subway over and wake up Phyllis and I'll show you what I'm doing instead of social work. You like?"

"Like. But what about Kincaid?"

"He's kind of worried," she admitted.

"How long have the papers been—uh—missing?" It was almost like old times. Years before, in college, Jo-Anne had always confided her pranks to me. Someone had to tell her when to call it quits, and in those days I had usually taken the job upon myself.

"Just three days, Jase. He's absent-minded and still thinks they've just been misplaced and are going to turn up. Actually, it could be good publicity—if he calls the police, I mean. What do you think?"

"I think you ought to return the papers."

"Killjoy!"

"No, really. If it's like that Kinsey stuff, it could be dynamite."

"It's a little different—but dynamite, all right. Do you cheat on your income tax, Mr. Jones? When your wife spent a week at the orphanage with the Junior League, you didn't watch television, did you? Or, Mrs. Jones, when your husband went to that convention in Chicago, did you play canasta *every* night? Two hundred questions, Jase. Five hundred questionnaires. No wonder Doc is worried."

"You're some scientist," I said. "You better return them."

"Well, maybe. But let me show you anyhow. Unless you want to go back to bed."

"Alone?"

"Definitely alone. I'm a working gal." Jo-Anne squirmed out of my arms and headed for the door, blushing and smiling.

"Let's go take a look at those top-secret papers," I said. We linked arms and took the elevator to the ground floor and outstared the desk clerk who was burying his nose in the register when we left, to make sure I had registered single so he could snicker away the wee hours of the morning.

* * * *

We left the dusty subway smells at 116th Street, trading them for the damp cold of early February and the rain, softer now, dancing like confetti in the glare of the street lamps. Jo-Anne lived in an ancient apartment house midway between Columbia University and the Hudson River.

As we walked from the subway station, she chattered about the difference between the published Kinsey and the soon-to-be-published Kincaid. Kinsey attempted a nationwide survey but stopped with sex. Kincaid's study confined itself to New York City but otherwise was far more inclusive: it dug into sex, business ethics, social life, gambling, relations with the government and religion. Kinsey, never dreaming of best-seller fame at the beginning, had written long, essentially dull tomes. Kincaid had come down from his ivory tower and admitted with unpedantic cheer he was as guilty as any statistic in his book, but needed the money and wouldn't hide from the fame and sure, his *Twentieth Century Morality* would be sensational. "Just the same, he's being very conscientious and scientific about the whole thing," Jo-Anne assured me, as we rode up in the creaking, self-service elevator.

Maybe the building was old, but the walls of the ninth floor were nicely decorated with framed water-colors and the floor was of cork tile. Indirect lighting suffused everything with a pinkish glow. Because of the hour, I found myself walking on tiptoe. "I hope this Phyllis doesn't mind my barging in like this," I said.

"Stop slinking like that," Jo-Anne said. "You could stamp your feet and it wouldn't be heard on this cork. And Phyllis will love you. She thinks it's time she got married."

"At three A.M.?"

"At any old time of any old day. Here we are."

Jo-Anne explored the pocket of her raincoat and emerged with a key which fit the lock of apartment 9-EL "Funny," she said. "The door isn't locked."

"So?"

"Phyllis always locks the door."

"Always?"

"I mean, when she's alone here. She's kind of a scaredy-cat that way."

"Maybe she's got company," I said.

"Well, come on, we'll see." She pushed open the door. I followed her into the dark apartment.

I closed my eyes, then opened them, but still could see nothing in the darkness. "I'll give us some light," Jo-Anne said.

Something rustled in the darkness in front of us. It might have been someone brushing his hand against the wall so he could feel his way toward the door.

Suddenly I had a feeling—not the kind of feeling you sometimes hear about, a premonition of things about to happen. A feeling, rather, that things had just happened, maybe only a moment or so before our arrival.

"Phyllis?" Jo-Anne called softly. "Phyl?"

I heard the click of a light switch. "Darn," Jo-Anne said. "The bulb must have blown. Phyllis, is that you?" No answer. "Didn't you hear something, Jase?"

"Yeah, I heard something."

My pupils had dilated and now I could vaguely make out Jo-Anne's form alongside me. Ahead was blackness.

"I'll put the light on in the living room," she said.

"No. Don't." Suddenly I was wary. The unlocked door, the light that wouldn't work, whoever it was inside the apartment that wouldn't answer when Jo-Anne called... I reached back of me, meaning to open the hall door and let the pink light enter the apartment.

"Phyl?" Jo-Anne whispered, her voiced edged thinly with fear. "Answer me, Phyl." Her hand found mine in the darkness and squeezed it. I turned and yanked at the door but whirled back to face the darkness of the apartment when footsteps thudded directly at me.

It took about a second to associate the dull *thunking* sound and the shattering with the pain which blossomed inside my head, reached the surface and exploded there. It took the same second for me to fold at the middle and the knees and sink to the floor. Jo-Anne was beginning to scream but I lost the sound somehow in a dull, distant roaring. Legs pounded over me. The door swung wide, then slammed. It was so dark it made no difference whether I shut my eyes or kept them open.

I shut them.

CHAPTER TWO

There was this whimpering which, I guessed, wouldn't stop until I could somehow manage to force my eyelids up and stare at something besides their unseen insides. There were sobs which went with the whimpering and said it was worse than just Jason Chase getting hit on the head, much worse. There were the sounds of a faucet running somewhere, the feel of something cold and wet against my forehead.

I opened my eyes. The light came down the length of a long foyer and there wasn't much of it, but too much under the circumstances. I blinked away the pain and tried again. This time I saw Jo-Anne squatting on her heels next to me, patting my forehead with a red-and-white washrag. The red was blood.

My hands found shards of crockery on the floor as I forced myself into a sitting position. It might have been a vase once but it had succumbed to my tough head, "Don't tell me that was Phyllis," I said.

It was a mistake. Jo-Anne dropped the washrag and instead of just whimpering, hysterically sobbed. Finally, she pointed one hand toward where the light was coming from. So I got up, patted her shoulder in a meaningless understanding gesture when I didn't understand at all, and staggered inside. Then I understood.

The light was emerging from a floor lamp in the living room. I saw an orange chair and a green one, a table-model TV set, a brown sectional sofa, an L-shaped coffee table and a cabinet which probably contained liquor.

I also saw the body of a young woman, almost certainly Phyllis Kirk, lying on the floor this side of the coffee table, where it had fallen after something much harder than the broken vase had crushed the back of her head, spilling blood on the gray twist carpet.

I walked into the kitchen and lit a match. The door of the fuse box set into the wall stood open. Probing with my fingers by the flickering match light, I found that two of the three fuses had been loosened in their sockets.

I screwed them down tight, then half-filled a tall glass with cold water from the tap Jo-Anne had left running, then found some rye in the living-room cabinet and filled the glass the rest of the way. I brought the drink to Jo-Anne in the foyer.

She was still sobbing into her hands and for the first time I saw the angry red welt alongside her ear where whoever had struck me with the vase had probably used his fist. "Drink this," I said. I got my hand under her chin and tilted her head up. She looked at me and through me and through the wall behind me, but when I said "drink this" again she obediently took the glass in both hands like a little girl, leaning back with it and not pausing until it had been emptied. It went down like water and had about the same effect as water, not even changing the lack of expression in her eyes or the way she was crying again after the glass was empty.

Finally she said, "I killed her. The Kincaid papers are gone. It's just like I hit her and killed her."

"How do you know they're gone?"

"She—she had one page in her hand. The last page—crushed—like she was trying to hold on to them. I thought it was all so funny, Jase. I killed her. Phyllis." She handed me a crumpled sheet of paper.

"I'd better call the police," I said.

"Call anyone you want. I don't care." The crying would stop and the talking would start, then the talking would stop and the crying would commence again. Now she talked. "You can get out of here, Jase," Jo-Anne said. "You're an ex-convict. You'll be under suspicion as soon as they see your record. Just go away and don't come back. I'll be all right. I'll be fine." And the crying.

Jo-Anne getting into hot water over her practical jokes. And me making like a boy scout and getting her out. Just like old times long ago in school, before Ken and Julia and jail. "I'll never send you away," I said, "remember? How about vice-versa?"

"But the police."

"Remember?"

"I remember, Jase. I'm cold. Just hold me, that's all. Hold me, hold me, hold me—God, poor Phyllis."

She was having the shakes suddenly. Shakes, shivers, rattling teeth. I tried to warm her but it was no good. I put my damp trenchcoat aside and draped my jacket across her shoulders, but that didn't help either. I found the phone and called the police.

She was still shaking and chattering when they came. The first to arrive was the two-man team of a prowl car which happened to be in the neighborhood and probably got alerted via its squawk box. The sergeant had a dour face and a body so thin the police overcoat looked like a tent. His partner adjusted the ear flaps of his cap, then took the whole contraption off his head and scratched at thinning, sandy hair. "Did you say murder?"

"Inside," I told him, and waited.

The sergeant tried to comfort Jo-Anne by giving her the there-there-everything's-going-to-be-all-right-now line, but she kept right on crying like she'd forgotten how to do anything else.

The sandy-haired cop returned from the living room. "It's a floater, Jimmy," he said in a flat, awed voice. "We'd better call in."

Sergeant Jimmy nodded, and I offered sandy-hair a cigarette. He got it lit on the second try with trembling fingers, and even if all the detective stories you ever read tell you that a prowl-car crew makes like a couple of hawkshaws, don't you believe it. Where homicide's involved, they suddenly become uniformed messenger-boys, because this business of homicide is specialized.

I knew, because the man who might have been my father-in-law but was my brother's father-in-law instead was a detective lieutenant at Homicide Squad, Manhattan West, which works out of the West 20th Street Precinct. I began to hope Pop Grujdzak would be home in bed snoring the night away, but since he'd always favored the swing shift I had my doubts.

Sergeant Jimmy was saying, "Here's where we break up a mess of all-night domino games. You go downstairs and call in, George." George went. I knew that the call would go to George's local precinct, to the police medical examiner, to the crime photographic bureau and to one of Manhattan Island's two murder teams, Homicide Squad, Manhattan West, where Pop Grujdzak worked.

"Let's go into the kitchen," Sergeant Jimmy said. Between us, we got Jo-Anne to her feet. Sergeant Jimmy drew her a glass of cold water and said nothing when I spiked it with rye. We watched her drink it down without blinking, then I stared at the cracked plaster above the stove and the grease stains on the white wall and the clock-radio on one side of the Formica table while Sergeant Jimmy asked some routine questions and did some scribbling on a pad so he'd have something to show the boys from Manhattan West.

"Did she live alone?"

"No. With Jo-Anne Stedman here."

"And she was?"

"Phyllis Kirk."

"Family?"

"Ask Jo-Anne."

Jo-Anne went on crying, silently.

"What happened to your head?"

"A guy came running out and slugged me."

"See him?"

"Uh-uh."

"The girl see him?"

"Search me."

"What's your name?"

"Jason Chase."

"Relative?"

"Friend of Miss Stedman."

"Where do you work?"

"Unemployed."

Sergeant Jimmy chewed on his pencil, considering. "Care to explain that?"

"Prison," I said. "I just got out."

The way he was chewing, he'd need a new pencil soon. "What for?"

"Rent gouging and other equally well-thought-of real estate practices."

"You trying to be funny?"

"Truth, Sarge."

"How long?"

"Two years."

"A lot of gouging."

"Yeah," I said.

"He's all right," Jo-Anne said with utterly no expression. I hadn't thought she was listening. "We spent the whole night together in his hotel room."

"Well, now," said Sergeant Jimmy. Jo-Anne was a looker, harlequin glasses or no. It would be something to tell the boys at the precinct. "What time did you get here?" asked Sergeant Jimmy.

"After three."

"The door was open," Jo-Anne told him. "Phyllis always locks it. Someone ran at us in the darkness and hit us. I didn't see him."

"Miss Kirk get along with people?"

"Yes," Jo-Anne said. "She's—was—easy-going. Never argued about anything."

"No enemies?"

"She never told me of any."

"What did she do?"

"Research assistant for Dr. Coleman Kincaid over at the University."

Sergeant Jimmy stood up and rubbed his bony hands together. He probably had visions of Communist, subversives. "Doing government work?"

"Afraid not," I said.

"Sociology," Jo-Anne told the sergeant.

"Oh." Sergeant Jimmy's stomach grumbled and he looked at Jo-Anne in embarrassment. "Heck," he said.

Jo-Anne went to the sink and washed her face, drying it with a dish towel hanging on a chrome rack on the door of the broom closet. "I'll make some coffee if you want. Instant stuff."

"Do that," I said. She hadn't said a word to the cops about her practical joke.

Jo-Anne had started pouring the coffee when the doorbell rang. After four in the morning, it would be either the milkman or cops. I was not betting on Louis Pasteur's boy. We all deserted the kitchen for the front door.

"Police Medical Examiner," the stocky man with rimless glasses and a doctor's satchel told us. "This the right place?"

"Come in."

For a while I watched him scurry about Phyllis Kirk's body on all fours like a spider, then I returned to the kitchen.

Buzz went the doorbell again.

This time it was three men from the photographic bureau. Complete with cameras, flash attachments and light-meters. "Hello, Sidney," the M.E. greeted one of them, scurrying back into the foyer. "She's in there."

Sidney yawned, revealing crooked yellow teeth. "Out of bed they got me," he said, and led his safari into the living room.

These were the specialists and murder was their stock in trade. Sergeant Jimmy might be a novice, but not these boys.

And certainly not Pop Grudjzak, who tried his thumb on the doorbell next. He entered, stared at me, and something behind his small eyes under the jutting ridges of his brows went silently click, click, click and the thin lips hardly moved but he said, "Jason Chase," clearly and distinctly in a way which would have made his elocution teacher happy.

Detective Lieutenant Emil Grujdzak, called "Ears" by the underworld but not to his face, was a huge man. Not fat, just big all over, with a bald dome of a head and ears like taxicab doors someone forgot to close. All the features of his face—the shrewd small eyes under craggy brows, the miniature flat nose which belonged to a bantam-weight and not a heavy, the round pursed lips—could have fit easily on one hemisphere of a good-sized orange. But the rest of Pop Grujzak was huge.

"Jason Chase," he said again, through still-pursed lips. His voice was a deep rasp, but not loud. In the old days, Julia had told me, a thug had socked him one in the Adam's apple and he hadn't been able to talk so good since then. "I didn't know you were out."

"I'm out," I said. "How's the family?"

He ignored me and turned to Sergeant Jimmy, who'd come trotting out into the foyer when he heard Pop Grujzak's rasp. "I see the M.E. and the pinup detachment are here."

"Yes, sir, Lieutenant. I've made a preliminary investigation for you, and—"

"Thank you." Pop Grudjzak took the sergeant's pad, scanned it and said, "Thou shalt not kill…Thou shalt not commit adultery. It looks like you're using one to alibi the other, Chase." Pop was a frustrated revivalist, I'd always thought. Most homicide cops rarely make moral judgments, but Pop made them all the time and quoted the Bible so you couldn't argue with him. He thought he could cure the disease of murder by rubbing people's noses in it.

"Suppose you leave Miss Stedman out of this," I said. Pop's two assistants, both in plainclothes as he was, had gone inside to examine the body and the murder scene. Pop's specialty was people. Living people. "Well, now," he told me, "I can't very well do that, can I? She was the dead girl's roommate, according to the sergeant. She found the body. She provided you with an alibi."

"Since I never met Miss Kirk and have no motive, I don't see why I need an alibi."

"Miss Stedman," Pop said, "what kind of work were you and the deceased doing for this Dr. Kincaid?"

Jo-Anne had followed Sergeant Jimmy from the kitchen. "Interviewing people."

"Interviewing like Kinsey?" He snapped the words out electrically.

"Something like that. But how—"

"I read about Dr. Kincaid in the papers. Tell me, Miss Stedman, could someone have changed his mind about the interview and wanted his life story back?"

"We'd have given it to him in that case," Jo-Anne told him. "This work is entirely voluntary."

"Would some of the material have been embarrassing?"

"Very."

"It was kept under lock and key?"

"Coded."

"Where?"

Jo-Anne gulped air and leaned against me. She was cold all over. "At the laboratory and at Dr. Kincaid's home in Putnam County."

"Listen, Pop," I said. "She's had a shock, so why don't you leave her alone for the time being?"

"It's Lieutenant Grujdzak, Chase. I'll tend to my own business and expect you to do the same. Anywhere else, Miss Stedman?"

"Not ordinarily."

"What do you mean, 'not ordinarily'?"

"Well, just not." Jo-Anne's voice was pitched nervously high and came close to breaking now.

"Now, miss."

"She told you," I said.

"Chase."

"She needs rest, Lieutenant. Why don't you have the M.E. look at her?"

"Chase!"

"Hell, leave her be."

"*Chase!*"

Rasp, rasp, rasp.

"Leave him alone," Jo-Anne sobbed. "He's got nothing to do with this."

"Prove it"

"I already said I was with him—"

"In bed, yes," Pop rasped. "You could be alibi-ing each other."

"He has no interest—"

"Miss Stedman," said Pop's voice. His eyes slid shut. "Suppose you let me decide that."

"I know all about you, Mr. Grujdzak," Jo-Anne said. "How you didn't want Jase to go near that precious daughter of yours, or Jase's brother, either. They weren't good enough. No one was good enough. She had an Electra complex a mile long and you liked it fine. You liked it even better when Jase went to jail, but she married his older brother. You'd like to get back at Jase for that, too, wouldn't you? Wouldn't you?"

"My dear Miss Stedman, I'm not being interrogated here, you are. And your ex-convict friend."

"Then listen to me. Last Saturday I took some of Dr. Kincaid's papers for his book from the University laboratory and brought them here. Doc is absent-minded and a worry wart so we thought—"

"Who is we?"

"Phyllis and I. We thought it would be a great joke.

"A great joke…"

"You don't have to, Jo," I said. "He can't pin this one on me even if he wanted to. They saw me at the hotel. They saw both of us. The room clerk."

"That's all right," Jo-Anne said. "We kept the papers here and Doc got frantic, looking all over. We kept on laughing behind his back. Maybe it wasn't funny, like a hotfoot that ruins a good pair of shoes, but once we started, we didn't want to stop."

"And where are the papers now, Miss Stedman?"

"I don't know. I don't know where. They were stolen. Whoever killed Phyllis…stole them," Jo-Anne finished lamely.

Pop Grujdzak lit a cigarette and let the smoke trickle through his nose. "Practical joke," he said. "Some practical joke. Maybe the law won't see it this way, Miss Stedman, but you are as guilty as the man who sneaked up behind your roommate and split her skull open. In the eyes of the Lord you are guilty of murder. Of murder, Miss Stedman." The revivalist fire was in his eyes, burning bright but ugly.

I said, "She doesn't have to take that."

The M.E. scurried out into the foyer, closing his satchel. "I'll send for the meat wagon to take her to the morgue, Lieutenant. Her skull was crushed between two and three A.M., maybe a little later. No signs of struggle, so it probably came as a surprise to her."

Pop nodded his bald dome. "Tell me, Miss Stedman, if someone got hold of those papers, could he use them for blackmail?"

"You mean to blackmail Dr. Kincaid?"

"No. The people you interviewed."

"Not unless the code could be broken. It's a safeguard always used in this type of research."

"Who knows the code?"

"Phyllis knew it. I know it, and Dr. Kincaid."

"Who else was aware you had the papers here, besides Chase?"

"No one. And Jason didn't know. That's the truth. Not until I told him about it at his hotel."

"Then he did know."

"We came straight here together and found Phyllis…dead."

"Maybe she told someone, then. Incidentally, how do you know the papers are missing?"

"She found this," I said. I took the sheet of paper from my pocket. *Page 768*, it said in the upper left-hand corner. It was filled with typed letters in meaningless combinations, but strung together like words in sentences and paragraphs. Someone had scrawled a telephone number in pencil on the reverse side. It was a Plaza exchange and I memorized it before surrendering the paper to Pop Grujdzak.

"What's this number?" Pop asked Jo-Anne.

She looked at it. "I don't know, but it's Phyllis' writing, I think."

"Interesting," said Pop. He stalked inside to the living room and sprawled his big frame on the orange chair, watching his team at work, watching the photographers retrieving their flash bulbs from the floor, giving the huddled corpse we could hardly see from out here in the foyer a quick examination.

"If they could break the code," Pop said to Jo-Anne. "Yes. They could use it for blackmail, then."

"We got more fingerprints," one of Pop's assistants said. "All over the place."

"Fine. Chase's will be on file with the Bureau of Criminal Identification. Won't they, Chase?"

"Yes."

"You can go now, in that case. But stay where we can keep in touch."

"I'm at the Madison Square Hotel," I told him.

"Registered under your own name?"

"That's right. Listen," I said, "if she's the only one besides Kincaid who knows the code, Jo-Anne might be in danger."

"Don't tell me my business."

"Don't worry about me," Jo-Anne said hurriedly. "I'll stay with Dr. Kincaid and his family up in Putnam."

"They'll be guarded by a plainclothes team if the Putnam County sheriff approves, Chase. Satisfied?"

I said I was but wondered why Pop had bothered to tell me.

"Just so you don't get any ideas," he went on. "They'll be guarded around the clock."

"Maybe you'd better book me," I challenged him.

"Maybe we'd better let you run around instead, Chase. So you can keep looking for trouble. The sooner you get back in jail, the better I'll like it. And that no-good brother of yours, my son-in-law."

Well, I couldn't argue with him. Ken had been guilty of a crime and I'd taken the rap for him.

"You're free. A free man. Go out and celebrate. Go ahead, why don't you? But count the days, Chase. We'll get you. Sneeze in the subway and we'll get you for spitting." His raspy voice had lowered to a whisper now. It sounded like he had cancer of the throat; I wondered how many people would have minded. "Raise your voice and it'll come out assault. Pass a red light and we'll get your license for it. I'll see you, Chase. I sure will."

They were mean, empty threats. Pop Grujdzak was a homicide lieutenant and probably wouldn't see me again unless I bumped into another corpse. Or stuck my nose into police business by calling that Plaza phone number.

"One more thing, Chase. I don't want you bothering my daughter, understand?"

I grinned at him and stared him down. "Are you kidding? She happens to be my sister-in-law."

"I mean my other daughter."

"Who? Oh—you mean Stephanie? Why, she's a—a kid. I hardly know her!"

Jo-Anne stood on tiptoe and pecked at my lips. I said, "I'm going to call Dr. Kincaid's place later today. Where is he, Mahopac?"

"Mahopac."

"You better be there, Jo. Don't get loose, as the officer said. Stay close to home till this thing blows over."

"I've got to know."

"Jo," I said.

"You heard him, Jase. I'm guilty, morally. He said so."

"What does he know about it? Just stay put."

"Goodbye, Jase."

I headed for the door.

CHAPTER THREE

At the hotel, I took a few hours of sleep and a shave, then tried my luck in the coffee shop downstairs. Sipping coffee, I meditated on that Plaza Number.

Hell. I'd call the number later in the morning and see which branch of Murder, Inc. answered. But first I'd visit my brother and his loving wife at home.

Outside, a weak sun struggled with the cold February air and pale, harried subway folk were being disgorged by the kiosks onto the chilly sidewalks. I walked east.

The building in which Ken lived was a couple of blocks north of the Waldorf Astoria. A liveried doorman admitted me with a patronizing smirk which said my trench-coat and hatless head rated the front entrance only by a whisker or because the old lady had fixed him a good breakfast that morning.

The sixth-floor hallway sported an ankle-deep carpet of green and paler green walls and a green-tinted ceiling. It was like swimming in the Gulf Stream, except that the doors were starkly white. No. 602 belonged to Kenneth Chase.

But Mrs. Kenneth Chase answered the door.

"Jason," she said.

I couldn't shut my mouth, either. She'd hardly changed at all, not unless you counted the faint, disillusioned lines etched on either side of her mouth. She was a small brunette, round enough so you'd want to reach out and touch but not so much that you'd call her plump. Her hair was pulled back in a long bob and the wide eyes were dark brown and enormous and looked completely without guile, but she could out-guile Lucrezia Borgia if she set her mind to it. She wore a peignoir which seemed to be made of countless layers of tinted smoke, and a lot of men seeing her like that would wish for a stiff wind.

"Come on in, Jason. Ken's already left for the office."

"I wanted to see him."

"Well, have one drink with me, for old time's sake?"

"It's nine o'clock," I said. "In the morning."

Julia grinned. "Coffee, then," she said.

She gave me barely enough room to walk by her, my elbow stirring the smoky peignoir. She smelled of musky perfume and whisky. She closed the door behind her and leaned against it, grinning at me. She didn't have a load on, but she was well under way. I wondered how she'd be by cocktail time.

"Let me look at you, Jason."

I removed my trenchcoat. "How's your sister?"

"Stephanie? Oh, all right, I guess. I don't see too much of her."

"Julia, I ought to go down to Ken's office."

"What's the matter?"

"Nothing's the matter. Don't you have a maid or something?"

"Quit last week. Good ones are hard to find. Something bothering you, Jason?"

"Nope."

"I can tell."

"Well, Julia," I said, "What the hell do you think? I went off to jail to earn us a hundred thousand, so you married the guy. My brother."

Julia smiled and sat down on a sofa which was squat Chinese Modern and expensive. "I'm glad you still feel that way about me."

"I don't feel any damn way at all about you."

Julia trickled three ounces of whisky from a decanter on the cocktail table into a water tumbler and drank it like tea. When I had known her, she would take an occasional nip, that was all. "Sit down, Jason. I'll get the coffee."

"I just had some. Julia, I ought to—"

"Be going now? Jason, I believe you're afraid."

So I snorted and plopped down next to her on the Chinese Modern, crossing my legs primly. Suddenly Julia's arms looked for and found each other behind my back and Julia's face floated toward mine, the lips wet and slack and very red, and Julia's voice scratched out "Jason Jason Jason" on a broken record.

She is going to kiss me, I thought, and this was one hell of a note, my sister-in-law. But she didn't make it. Instead, she started to cry, not like Jo-Anne after she had found Phyllis' body, but loud and blubbery and drizzling tears on my shoulder.

"It was a mistake, Jason," she blubbered. "A stupid mistake. I should have waited, I should have realized Ken would be like that, wanting me only because you already had me. He doesn't love me at all—he couldn't love anyone but himself, ever, except as part of himself like his feet or his hands."

"Hey, take it easy," I said. "I don't want to hear this—"

"You were no good for me, he said. You were shiftless. He took you in and gave you a job or you'd still be wandering. You didn't take any rap for him, like you told me. It was all your own fault, everything. You were no good. First he took me out just to cheer me up, then more, then every night, and he kept on lying and I'm weak, Jason." Still crying, still drunk, she shrugged her white arms and fleshy smooth shoulders and stood up, the peignoir parting and partially falling from her creamy body.

Maybe it was in my eyes, the way I felt, the way I couldn't help staring at her as if she were something not entirely clean, although beautiful. She whirled and let herself fall to the sofa, shaking with sobs. "He doesn't love me," she said. "He doesn't even make love to me now, Jason. I'm human. I'm a woman. He's unfaithful. He flaunts it and says why don't you get a divorce? But Pop won't take me back home…and I have no other place to go."

I stood up and put on my trenchcoat. I wanted to scrub myself with wire brushes. I said, "Why won't he take you back?"

"Me? Because I loved a convict—and married a convict's brother."

"Is that the whole of it? Or does Pop recognize what you are? Tell me, have you stuck to your own vows?"

"Jason, I wanted to wait for you. Oh, I did want…"

"I mean your marriage vows."

"You're taking his side. Come here and touch me, Jason. That's all I ask. Just touch me, and then say what you want." She rolled over and propped herself up on one elbow, the peignoir clutched in a white-knuckled fist in front of her breasts.

Hell, she'd twisted the knife in me while I was behind bars. I turned and headed for the door.

CHAPTER FOUR

"I want to see Mr. Chase," I told the receptionist half an hour later. I didn't recognize her, nor any of the other employees in the outer office of Chase Construction and Management Corporation. Apparently Ken had made a complete housecleaning after the D.A. had settled for the younger of the two Chase brothers.

"Have you an appointment?"

"Yes," I said softly. "I made it more than two years ago."

Brown eyes widened. "Would that be Jason Chase, sir?"

"You've got it," I admitted, then watched her flick the intercom nervously.

"It's your brother!" she cried. "I mean, Mr. Jason Chase to see you, sir."

I'll grant him this—he didn't make me cool my heels. A moment later I took a deep breath and opened the door marked *KENNETH LAMAR CHASE, President.*

Ken is big, my height or a little taller. You'd call him self-indulgently handsome, with a look of slight, socially acceptable dissipation in the eyes and around the petulant, down-drooping mouth. His hair is gray at the temples but otherwise black as my own.

He came around the big oak desk in a hurry, favoring his game leg with more of a limp than was necessary, his face thawing slowly into a big smile which exploded into booming laughter when he reached me. He whacked my back soundly with a slab of a hand. "Jason, boy!" he said, still booming, "Let me look. There, hold it. Stand back. The same. The very same boy, my brother. It almost makes me want to cry."

The first and last time I had seen Ken cry was twenty years before in Vermont—when he had been fifteen and I had been ten. The snow had come down that day clean and white, not dirty gray like in the city, mantling the mountains with a dazzling, sun-brilliant cloak by midafternoon. Ken had stood at the top of the slope, anxious on his skis, leaning forward and bending at the knees as we'd been taught. "Track," he hollered, and "track, here I come!"

Then came one of those crazy impulses which sometimes strike a ten-year-old boy and make him uniquely dangerous. I'd reached out with both hands and shoved against Ken's bright plaid mackinaw and yelled, "Look out below!" and then, horrified, watched Ken tumble down the long steep slope, skis twisting and spinning like the spokes of a wheel, kicking up a great spray of white snow as he rolled and furrowed and fell down-slope. He wailed all the way down and was still wailing when I reached him.

The doctors did what they could, but he'd had a nasty double compound fracture of the right leg, the bones jutting through his blue ski-togs so white and sharp I got ill and threw up. He walked with a limp after that and I used to carry his books to school, and fight his fights for him, and bring him things when he wanted, them—like hot drinks in bed even long after he had got well. I must have looked so mournful when it happened, our folks hadn't even touched me or scolded me or anything. Sometimes I used to wish they'd whaled the tar out of me, so I wouldn't have to go on expiating all the rest of my life.

"Hello, Ken," I said now, bringing myself back to the office. "I came to see you." Of course I came to see him. It didn't have to be said. Ken always made me self-conscious and unsure of myself.

"Will you use the money to go into competition with me, Jase boy? Construction could stand some young blood. Shot in the arm, you know."

"No. I came to see you about that. The money."

"No mix-up, is there? I—"

"Uh-uh. I got it. I don't want it." Those were the words, four of them. Take the rap for him and lose two years and accept no payment so maybe you can even things out some and put the shoe on the other foot. I didn't feel good saying it, though. Indifferent.

Ken thumped my back again and ran his tongue around the first layer of a cigar before he poked it into his mouth and set fire to it. "Always the joker," he said.

"Not any more. Not in twenty years." I'd learned about jokes. So had Jo-Anne, I thought sadly. Back at school I had kept trying to tell her, warn her.

Ken was talking. "What then? Isn't it enough?"

"Plenty."

"Julia? You're bitter about Julia?"

I shook my head.

"You agreed to take the money then, Jason. Two years ago."

"I grew up." I pulled the check from my pocket and tore it without looking at it, letting the pieces flutter to the floor and scatter there.

"I don't consider this final," Ken told me. "I'll write another any time you say. I am sorry about Julia, Jason. One of those things."

"You should be sorry."

"She knew what she was doing. She made up her own mind—"

"Oh, hell, come off it," I said. "I'm not talking about that. I mean Julia herself. You ought to divorce her, if that's what she wants."

"She doesn't want. Not really. You saw her, Jason?"

"Ken, you haven't changed at all. But Julia. Julia's changed."

"I'll admit she's a candy-eater and has put on a few pounds, but..."

"I'm not talking about that."

"What did she tell you?"

"She didn't have to say a word."

"That she was unfaithful, perhaps? That I love her as much as when I married her a year ago, but she went to bed with another man who'd planned the whole thing and got pictures and is blackmailing us now? Did she tell you that?"

More blackmail? "No," I said. "She didn't tell me."

"Maybe I shouldn't tell you either, Jason. I shouldn't bother you. You're all mixed up. You've got your own problems."

"I'm listening," I said.

"Well, there are two sides. If he'd stop bothering us, though, I'm sure everything would be all right again. Everything would be fine." Ken rolled smoke around in his mouth and stared at the glowing tip of his cigar. "I shouldn't tell you all this."

"What's his price?"

"Whatever he needs. It changes. It never stops. I've got to pay him, Jason. The scandal. The disgrace. I have a private detective on it, but..." Ken suddenly slapped the desk with a broad palm. "Tell me, Jason. Now that you're out, what are you going to do?"

"I haven't decided yet."

"Then come to work for me."

"You can shove it," I said.

"Now wait a minute. I don't mean for the construction company. You've had enough and I don't blame yon. I mean that you could work on this thing, this awful shakedown ruining Julia and me. Put the fear of God into him, Jason. You're big and strong. You're no cripple." Ken limped around the desk and sat down. The heel of his right shoe was built up to support a twisted leg.

"You mentioned a private detective," I said.

"It's not personal with him," Ken pleaded. "He acts strictly within the law. It's just another fee to him. But you—I mean, you could get those negatives for me if anyone could."

"I'm a convict," I said. I was thinking of Pop Grujdzak. "If I sneeze in the subway they'll get me for spitting."

"Blackmail is illegal, don't forget. He won't go crying to the cops."

"Who is he?"

"Then you'll do it?"

"I'm just asking."

"His name is Wompler, Wilson Wompler. A publisher of magazines. Girlie-sheets, I believe. You know, *Giggle* and *Vamp* and those things for perverts. You'll do it?"

"I don't know. I want you to understand this, though. We're even, Ken. Finally even. Your leg, my two years. If I do it, it's a favor. Understand?"

"Anything you say."

"Good," I told him. I looked down at the torn pink scraps on the floor. "Better get rid of that garbage."

* * * *

Ten minutes later I was downstairs in a drugstore, making myself at home in the phone booth. The information operator gave me Coleman Kincaid's number in Putnam County and it was Jo-Anne who answered the phone. The Putnam County sheriff was allowing plain-clothesmen from New York to guard the Kincaids and Jo-Anne around the clock. She didn't know if she'd do anything foolish or not. It depended on what I meant by foolish. I didn't like the way she said that and figured she'd stay under lock and key only so long. I could call the number Phyllis Kirk had scrawled on the last page of the Kincaid papers and try to beat Jo-Anne to the punch, though.

Except that I had another call to make first. To a certain Guido Isaac. A runt who'd have trouble making five-five in elevator shoes. He'd been a kind of fringe figure, half-participant, half-spectator, in the heyday of the rackets, and had since and more recently been tempered by taxpayer justice up the river. One inmate there had found Guido Isaac a convenient outlet for suppressed aggressions, until one day I took the guy's side and knocked said inmate's teeth in. After that, Guido had sworn there was no favor he wouldn't do me, especially since I spent a few days in solitary for my ruckus. So now he was out and I was out, and I was thinking maybe he could help me after all.

"Hey, Guido," I said. "You'll never guess."

His voice almost jumped through the phone at me. "Jason! But you don't have to check. Like I told you, I'm going honest. Don't you worry."

"You're okay," I said. "But Guido. There's something. A guy named Wilson Wompler. Right. Find out about him. If he's been in numbers or the rackets or anything, I want to know."

Chirped Guido Isaac, "My pleasure."

"Thanks," I said. "I'll call you in a day or so, then we'll get together for a beer."

Call three was that Plaza number. I dialed it and scowled back through the dirty glass at the middle-aged woman who threatened to burst her corset stays with impatience while she waited for the phone. It buzzed twice in my ear and a sing-song voice sang, "Good afternoon. Wompler Publications."

"*Which* publications?" I gasped.

"Wompler Publications," she sang again.

"That wouldn't be Wilson Wompler?"

"*Giggle, Vamp, Peek-a-boo, Keyhole* and America's newest expose magazine, *Hush*. Wilson Wompler, publisher. Whom did you wish to speak to?"

I asked her where they were located and got the answer and hung up. I sat there staring at the phone until the middle-aged woman began to rap on the glass with her knuckles. Wilson Wompler was blackmailing my brother Ken because, allegedly, Wilson

Wompler had gone to bed with Ken's wife and could prove it. It was Wilson Wompler's business phone number which Phyllis Kirk had written down some time before she had been murdered. Coincidence? Probably, although it meant Mr. Wompler had his thumb up to the elbow in a couple of dirty pies. It looked as though the long arm of coincidence, if such it was, was driving me closer to Mr. Wilson Wompler with every breath I took.

"Sorry, lady," I told the middle-aged woman as I accordioned the booth door toward me and stood up.

This Mr. Wompler I'd have to see.

Chapter Five

Wompler's office was located east of Broadway on 44th Street. Loft space vied with dingy office suites in a ten-story structure which could use a sand-blasting on the outside and a lot else on the inside. The lobby was only a waiting room for the elevator, which had one of those old grille gates and an ancient operator with psoriasis or some nameless disease disfiguring his face. "Wompler," I said and we were on our creaky way up.

I went left down a peeling hallway to a double smoked-glass door which bore the legend *Wompler Publications* and under it a list of cheesecake magazines with only *HUSH* in capital letters.

The inside surprised me. Like Chippendale furniture in a tenement on Double Fifth Avenue, or lace curtains on the window of a garage. There were good reproductions of Utrillo and Matisse on the walls and a mobile hanging from the ceiling and amorphous amoebas of carpet on the floor, each supporting a modern furniture grouping in the large waiting room. And there was a receptionist who looked as if she'd stepped right off one of Wompler's magazine covers.

"I don't have an appointment," I told her, "but I think Mr. Wompler will see me. The name is Chase."

Smiling at me, the receptionist leaned forward to display more cleavage than the Breen Office considers digestible for the great twelve-year-old audience, plugged a line on her monitor board and announced me. A moment later she said, "Mr. Wompler is shooting a story now, sir. Set Five. He says for you to go right in."

"They ought to take pictures of you," I said. It seemed the proper thing.

"Oh, they do, sir, all the time."

And then I was across the reception room and pushing inside through a swinging door upon which the shadow of the mobile was cast, its darts and cones and cylinders spinning slowly in an unfelt wind.

* * * *

It was bedlam. Shirt-sleeved men sprinted back and forth shouting instructions. Strobe lights glared briefly, stark white, then faded. Wall partitions were being wheeled back and forth across the huge barn of a room, squeaking and teetering. But in the confusion you could see that each impermanent set had three walls and usually one or more female occupants.

Minsky would have given his eye teeth for all this pulchritude but I felt like a man who'd been struggling for ten days through desert sands, crying for water—and suddenly found himself inundated by a tidal wave. There was blonde hair, red hair, brown hair and black. Big girls, small girl, in-between girls. Girls wearing towels, bikini suits, spangles and G-strings, open vests, shorts or leotards. There were bosoms almost bare and bosoms barely supported and bosoms supported not at all but barely covered, sort of. There were curving thighs and sandaled feet and feet on spike heels and in hip-high leather boots. Altogether, square miles of posturing flesh.

Two chesty females in costumes mama never would have approved were staging a hair-pulling match before the camera on Set One. A dame in chains and a loose vest and not much else stared at the camera on Set Two, cringing before a background of minarets and towers painted on paper walls. Set Three was a studio beach, but the two girls thereon wore snips of cloth which bore the same relationship to the bikini bathing suit that the bikini bears to what grandmother wore on her trip to Atlantic City. A lone male model, apparently somewhat bewildered and wearing a tattered French Foreign Legion costume, was surrounded by a harem on Set Four.

Set Five was a boxing ring or wrestling ring, as the occasion demanded. Right now a tall and well-put-together representative of the fair sex, her skin oiled to look sweaty, was astride an unhappy-looking little man and in the process of spread-eagling him and pinning him to the canvas. The camera man darted in close and squawked, "More chest, more chest," then scrambled back to his camera. Strobes glared, the camera clicked, the strobes faded. Someone flung a large towel in the oily amazon's direction as she leaped to her feet and soon she was busy scrubbing the grease from her body.

The little man stood up, looking happy now. He supplemented his shorts and sneakers with a satin robe and smiled at me. "Nice, hey? Some set-up. Nice."

"What do you do when the postal inspectors come around?" I said.

"Oh, God," he cried. "Don't tell me you're a new inspector?"

"Nope. The name's Jason Chase and I'm looking for Mr. Wompler."

"I'm Wompler, but there's some mistake here. When the girl said Chase…"

"You were expecting my brother, Ken."

"You're his brother? Well, now. His brother." Wompler was about five-six and a hundred-thirty pounds sopping wet, but if the gals still go for the ectomorphic type, he was handsome. He had wavy brown hair which he was busy combing now, wide-spaced eyes, gaunt cheeks and a lower lip currently on the verge of a pout.

"It's about Ken's wife," I said.

"I'll bet you're wondering, hey?"

"Why should I wonder?"

"I mean, me modeling. The model didn't show up, the male model. Had to take his place, like in the old days before we had a big studio. Audrey, come here."

The amazon ambled in our direction like a female John Wayne, hitching up her abbreviated shorts self-consciously. She was my height, which is an even six feet, with long tawny hair hanging down to her shoulders but in need of a brushing at the moment. She had muscles across her shoulders and on her arms and thickening her long thighs like a strenuous ballet dancer's, but her face seemed almost demure. Nature had endowed her for this occupation but I guessed she'd rather model lingerie.

"Audrey," Wompler said, "I'd like you to meet Mr. Jason Chase."

"How do you do?" said Audrey in a small voice, offering me a large limp hand.

"Audrey here used to be a lady grappler until she found she could make good money modeling as a lady grappler but not really grappling."

Audrey blushed a furious scarlet. "It was a living," she said.

"But she was afraid it would ruin her face, so she came here," Wompler told me, then declared abruptly, "Ours is an audience of the frustrated and neurotic. Wompler Publications caters to all kinds of screwballs. But don't think all we do is this junk. *Hush* is different."

"Sure," I said.

"We tell the truth in *Hush*! Hence the name, see? It's uncensored. We're shooting for a million paid circulation with that one. As soon as we hit it, I'm going to sell all the cheesecake books and go classy. Office on Fifth Avenue, with plush carpets. No modeled pictures but the real thing, politics and nudists and socialites and subversives. You get the idea?"

"Hush," I said.

"You got it."

"About Ken's wife," I said. "I was wondering if we could talk somewhere."

"I got an office back here."

Wompler led the way and I heard Audrey padding after us in her sneakers like Mary's little lamb.

I followed Wompler into an office which contained a desk and two chairs. Audrey stood until I offered her my chair. She smiled so hard I thought she'd spit out all her teeth.

"Now then," Wompler said. "What can I do for you?"

"It's not for me. Can I talk?"

"Audrey, you mean? You can talk. My right arm, Mr. Chase."

"Listen, Wompler. My brother Ken went along with you because he had no choice. But there's a limit. You keep jacking up the ante with no end in sight."

"We all must have our little joke," Wompler told me and grinned. Audrey grinned in sympathy. I didn't. "Exactly what do you want, Mr. Chase?"

"The negative. And all the prints."

Wompler considered this and shrugged. "Are you kidding?"

"I don't know how long I'm going to be in town, Wompler. It depends. But while I'm here I'll have nothing to do but make things uncomfortable for you. Every hour. Every day. Unless you come across." I kept telling myself I wasn't very good at this sort of thing. It was the most feeble kind of bluff. It was bluff of the laughter-producing and throw-that-bum-out-of-here variety.

"Why didn't you say so?" Wompler asked me. "Why didn't you say you wanted it stopped? The blackmail." He shrugged again. "So I'll stop. You got any other problems?"

I studied him and saw nothing. I stared at Li'l Audrey. "The negative," I said.

But Wompler shook his head. "Oh, no. We'll let your brother Ken take care of that. I want to know I get out of this cleanly. You understand?"

It was reasonable. It was so reasonable it made absolutely no sense at all. I nodded and said, "I'll tell Ken." Wompler stood up and we shook hands. He offered me a cigarette and lit up for himself and Audrey. "Care to look through some of our sheets before you go, Mr. Chase?"

"There's something else."

"So I'm listening."

"What was your business with a girl named Phyllis Kirk?"

"Oh, God," said Wompler. "Don't tell me you too? Half the cops in New York saw me about Miss Kirk this morning. The lady wants to do a story for *Hush*, so sure I'm interested. She calls me once or twice and makes an appointment to come up here and see me. This morning she's supposed to come. But the cops get here instead and tell me last night she was murdered."

Audrey smoked her cigarette daintily and just looked at us.

"What kind of story was she going to do?"

"It's a tragedy," Wompler told me. "I mean, her dying like this. It was the kind of story could jack circulation up over a million with a little luck. You know, wrap a band around the magazine with big letters—*The Truth Behind The Kincaid Investigations*! She could write it too, that girl. You know what she did for a living? She worked for this professor, this Coleman Kincaid at the University."

"She said she'd write the story for you?"

"She said if the price was right."

"What did you offer her?"

"I'm not sure I should…"

"If the police know," I lied, "I'll know."

"One thousand dollars."

"She agreed?"

"She said she wanted to talk about it. I said fine."

"I guess you know the Kincaid papers are loose," I said.

"Loose?"

"Stolen. Why she was killed, Wompler."

Wompler appraised me with suddenly shrewd eyes, curtained behind wisps of cigarette smoke in the still air of the office. He started to say something, then changed his mind and waited for me to continue. Audrey just watched and waited. You could hear the sounds of the models and cameramen outside, the frenzied noise behind the cheesecake pictures.

"Only trouble is," I said, "they're useless to whoever took them. They're coded, did you know that? You've got to know the code to understand the papers."

"Where do you fit in all this?" Wompler asked.

"I happen to know the code," I said. Naturally, it was a lie. Jo-Ann knew the code, and Dr. Kincaid. No other living person. But Jo-Anne's conscience would be itching to do something if the police didn't find Phyllis Kirk's killer soon. I didn't know how Wompler figured in the set-up if at all, but he was my only lead. So I let him think I knew. It might make things a little safer for Jo-Anne, if and when.

"That's interesting," Wompler admitted. "Maybe you can do a story for me?"

"No, thanks. I'm not even sure Phyllis Kirk agreed to do it."

"Now wait a minute. Are you calling me a liar?"

"Not necessarily."

"I got nothing to hide."

"She was a scientist with a trust to keep. It doesn't figure."

"So that makes me a liar?"

"I'll draw my conclusions," I said easily. "You can draw yours."

"I think you better get out of here." Wompler's face had drained white. The pouting lower lip began to tremble. It must have been a signal for Audrey, who stood up and said, still ladylike, "You'd better go. His blood pressure, Mr. Chase."

"Well," I said cheerfully, "I'll tell Ken what you said. He'll be pleased."

"You just keep away from this place," Wompler said, almost pleading. "Calling me a liar!" I sneered at him and thought, Julia really had tumbled down if she had gone for this bird.

"Go on," Li'l Audrey said, flexing her muscles prettily. She made one hell of a bodyguard.

I marched out of there and back past sets One through Four, almost reaching the door. Almost but not quite.

"Jason! Oh, Jason Chase."

It was one of the girls in the harem set, waving at me and bouncing in my direction. I squinted as a strobe unit flashed off to the right. "Julia?" I gasped.

"I don't look *that* old, do I?"

Well, she did look like Julia. She wore her hair in the same long bob, an anachronism which didn't seem to disturb the harem photographer. She was not quite as plump and curved more subtly. You could tell it was real, all delightfully real, because what little material covered her breasts did not support them, and beneath was a long stretch of curves and skin clear down to a pair of black, spangled panties, and the flashing legs below them and the painted toenails. She reached me half-trotting and said, "I'm Stephanie, silly."

Julia's kid sister. Brother, it suddenly occurred to me I'd been in jail a long time. Stephanie used to wear bobby sox and was just beginning to draw whistles from the younger set of college boys down near Washington Square where the Grujdzaks lived when I lost Ken's fight with the law and said goodbye to all my friends.

"Pop would never approve," I said.

"It's a long story," Stephanie told me, then raised a slim finger to her lip and added, "Don't tell on me. Please."

"Not me," I said. "You don't have to worry."

"What are you doing here?"

"Maybe we'll trade stories, if you're all through at the harem for today."

"All through."

"Take you home?"

"Just let me change, Jason."

Then she was gone and I stood there facing the dressing room with my mouth open. This was coincidence, too? It just couldn't be. Or could it?

I meant to try and find out.

Chapter Six

"I see you still don't like subways."

"Hate 'em," I said. We'd climbed back to the street near Washington Square, were crossing it now and watching the old men in overcoats and scarves feeding peanuts to the pigeons.

Stephanie wore one of those nubby coats pinched tight at the waist and flaring below it. A beret perched jauntily atop her head. "I don't want you to think it's too awful," she said. "Me modeling like that."

"Fifteen bucks an hour minimum, isn't it? Even Pop shouldn't complain about that."

"Jason. Pop isn't so bad. You two never got along, did you?" Her lips worked, as if she couldn't make up her mind whether to go on talking. Then she blurted, "It isn't the money. I used to do freelance modeling for ad agencies, at the same pay. I don't need this."

"So?"

"So...I can't tell you all of it, Jason. Julia's in trouble, bad trouble. I'm trying to help her."

"She ask you to?"

"Yes."

"How old are you, Steffy?"

"I'm nineteen. Be twenty next month. St. Patrick's Day."

"And you know all about the birds and bees?"

"Jason," she scolded me, then smiled impishly.

"Look, I know about the trouble. Ken is being blackmailed because of something Julia did. Julia asked you to help her because Ken is probably driving her nuts about it, at meals and between meals and every time he sees her. What's Julia got on you, though?"

"She's my sister."

"Still, you shouldn't mess with things like blackmail. And what would Pop do if he found out?"

"He mustn't, Jason. Ever. Emma knows all about it, but she's different."

Emma was Pop Grujdzak's unmarried sister, living with the Grujdzaks in lieu of a mother. She'd always had a kind of maiden-aunt crush on me although she wouldn't admit it.

"You bet she's different," I said. "She's a human being." We crossed the street from the square and cut across the cobblestones to a narrow lane hemmed in and darkened by the drab bulks of four-story walkups. Come summer, the sidewalk artists would display their canvases here, but right now they were freezing in their cold-water flats and blowing on their hands so they could paint and the only people on the street were hurrying as fast as they could go. Including us.

She got her arm under mine and we were walking by the rows of tenements which seemed pasted there against the bleak sky. Pretty soon we reached one that looked like all the others, except there were curtains in most of the windows and Venetian blinds in some and no cracks in any of the glass you could see.

"Well, here we are," Stephanie told me. "Thanks for the trip home, Jason. Will I see you?"

"You going to forget about Wompler?"

"I...I'll ask Julia."

I rubbed my cold-numb hands together and said, "Pop?"

She shook her head. "Out, I think. Aunt Emma would love to see you."

Stephanie's soft voice and her frankness and that contagious grin of hers were like an unexpected taste of Florida sunshine there in Greenwich Village in February. I had to check with Jo-Anne and Guido Isaac before the day was over, but they could wait a few minutes and so could Ken. "You," I said, "are on."

Upstairs, I could smell Aunt Emma's cooking even before we reached the door. Hungarian goulash was her specialty and this smelled like specialty day.

There was Emma, now, standing in the doorway, her more than ample bosom effectively blocking a view of the apartment, her gray hair bunned behind her head, her eyes twinkling and maybe smarting some and her wide mouth with no lipstick broadening into a grin. "Jason!" she said, her voice high but flat. Stew ladle and all, her hand went to her bosom and clutched the flowered fabric of her print housedress. "Jason, this is a surprise." But then she was scowling and saying, "You know Pop doesn't want you around here. He doesn't even want to see his son-in-law, let alone you."

"I'll be in and out like this," I said, snapping my fingers.

"Any coffee?" Stephanie said.

"Any stew?" I added.

"Oh, you," said Emma, and melted, and moved aside to let us in. They had the same old enamel-topped table and four chairs in the front room, which was the kitchen, with three burners on the ancient gas stove fit and the magic aroma of Emma's cookery wafting up from three chipped porcelain pots. The steam radiator was thunking away in a corner and still needed adjustment. My coat joined Stephanie's in the closet and she came back to the kitchen wearing a black velvet skirt and a white jersey blouse which clung slightly as she puttered around the kitchen, in a coltish young-girl way, preparing the coffee.

I sat down at the table and stretched my legs out long and comfortably. I was getting a glow just looking at Stephanie.

Then the door opened and Pop Grujdzak stamped in out of the hallway.

"Down here on a call," he rasped, "and I thought some java… Chase! What—"

"Coffee," Stephanie said lamely.

I pushed the chair back and stood up. The ceiling light gleamed on Pop Grujdzak's bald dome as he removed his hat and said, "You can just get your coat."

"We met by accident uptown," Stephanie said. "Jason took me home, that's all."

"It isn't all. I warned him. Why must he bother both my girls, you tell me that? The Good Book says…"

"It's what you feel in your heart, too," Emma said softly. "Not only what you read. Anyone can read the words, Emil."

"Emma!"

Stephanie's eyes were saying, please get out, get out, please. I looked at her, then back at her father. For all this beauty, all that ugliness. Side by side, the way of the world.

"You'd better go," Emma told me, sullen now. "You have no business here." She got my coat and gave it to me. Stephanie was standing in front of the stove with her back to us, not moving.

"That girl ought to be spanked," Pop said. If he wasn't so deadly serious, the small eyes staring straight ahead, unblinking, the voice a dry, throat-injured rasp, it would have been funny.

"She's a grown woman," I bristled. "You can't…"

"In my house, Mr. Chase, and with my girls, I can and I will. Anything the Good Lord tells me is right. Now get out."

"Maybe that's why Julia's a drunken tramp," I said softly. A silence filled the room. Stephanie whirled around and faced me, one fist clenched in front of her mouth, her breasts rising and falling rapidly under the white jersey blouse. Emma glared at me, then at Pop, and shook her head. It was a spiteful thing to say, but the words were out and I couldn't retract them. I shrugged into my coat and headed for the door, wondering how long they'd stand that way, like statues.

Pop bellowed and I spun toward him in time to see his great hammer of a fist blurring at me. I kept spinning and caught it on the side of my jaw and went numb all over, not hurt, but numb, slamming back against the shut door and sliding down into a sitting position while the door shuddered some in its frame behind me. I rubbed my knuckles against my lips and they came away red. Then the strength flowed back into me until I exploded with it all at once, leaping to my feet and roaring back at him. But Stephanie got between us, not facing her father, facing me. "I'll walk you downstairs, Jason," she said. "Right now. Please."

"You'll not leave this room," Pop rasped at her.

"Come on," Stephanie said, taking my arm. I wasn't trembling, she was.

"You can't come back here, then," Pop told her.

"Emil, now Emil," Emma said.

"It's all right, Steffy," I grinned, and chucked her one playfully on the jaw. "I deserved that."

I closed the door behind me and took the stairs down two at a time.

CHAPTER SEVEN

Walking back toward Washington Square as snowflakes started to swirl out of the darkening sky, I couldn't even find room inside me to hate Pop Grujdzak, not with thoughts of Stephanie filling me to bursting. But there were other things, so many other things which demanded attention in this cockeyed world. Was it only last night, less than twenty-four hours ago, that Jo-Anne had met me in the Madison Square Hotel? Was it this very morning that we had found Phyllis Kirk's body?

There was a drugstore off one corner of the Square, its lights warm and bright through the snowy murk. Inside, I found a booth and called Dr. Kincaid's number. A strange voice answered.

"This is Jason Chase," I said. "Dr. Kincaid?"

"Speaking."

"Doc, I hope you're not too sore at Jo-Anne for walking out with those papers. She's a great practical joker—I don't know, almost pathological with her. But she didn't mean any harm—"

"Chase, I'm a social psychologist. I know enough about people to understand they have all kinds of quirks. I couldn't be 'sore' at Jo-Anne for being herself. But I do regret the tragedy. Phyllis was a fine girl, one of the finest." His voice broke, but I didn't interrupt. After a moment, he asked, "Now, what can I do for you?"

"I'd like to talk to Jo-Anne, please."

"But Mr. Chase, we were hoping you'd know where she was."

"What's that?"

"Jo-Anne is gone. She left earlier this afternoon."

"The police—'"

"Were given the slip, as the expression goes."

"Damn!" I swore. "That crazy gal. Have they notified the New York cops?"

"I think so. We assumed Jo-Anne had gone to meet you."

"Uh-uh. Did she make any phone calls?"

"That's impossible to say. There's an extension in her room, you see."

"Weren't the cops monitoring phone calls?"

"Only incoming ones, I believe."

"If you get word from Jo-Anne, please call my brother's place and leave a message for me." I gave him Ken's Park Avenue number. "I'll be looking for her, Doc."

"Keep in touch."

I mumbled something and hung up, dialing Ken's business phone as soon as I could deposit another dime and get a dial tone.

"Hey, Ken," I said. "Jase. Wompler's agreed to stop blackmailing you."

"That's wonderful, boy! Good old Jason."

"You'll have to pick up the pictures yourself, he said. It was so easy, maybe I ought to go into the business."

"Julia and I will always be grateful, Jason. Provided Wompler's on the level."

"What do you mean?"

"He's cagey. Could be he just wanted to get you out of his hair. He didn't surrender the negative or the prints, don't forget."

"Yeah, but…"

"I'm not saying he pulled a fast one on you. I'm saying he might have. We're grateful either way."

"Listen," I said, "you mentioned a private detective this afternoon. Working on the case for you? Well, I'd like to see him."

"Not about Wompler?"

"Something else."

"Tad Barrett's the name. 1675 Broadway."

"You think he's good?"

Ken paused to consider. Then, "As good as any, probably. Those snoopers are too detached and impersonal."

"Just what I want. And Ken, you or Julia might be getting a call for me at your apartment. It's important."

"We'll take the message. But say, boy, why don't you come on over to our place till you get things straightened out for yourself? We've got plenty of room and it beats any flea-bitten hotel…"

"No, I couldn't."

"I insist, boy. Least I can do. What do you say?"

"Well, no. Thanks, Ken, but no."

"You want to hire Barrett for something? What are you going to pay him with, promises? Tell him to put it on my bill, Jason. Then come on over here to live. My own brother, it's the least I can do. I'll tell Julia to get one of the guest rooms ready. What do you say?"

Maybe he was really trying to do the right thing. It was a peace gesture, anyway. I said, "Okay, Ken. You twisted my arm."

Then I was outside in the snow looking for a subway to take me uptown to Barrett's. We had the guy surrounded, whoever he was. Manhattan West probably had half a hundred detectives canvassing the flats in Phyllis Kirk's neighborhood. Guido Isaac was digging into Wompler's past for me. I was trying to play footsie with the killer in my own way, and so was Jo-Anne. Now I'd usher in a well-recommended private cop and we'd have our killer good and hemmed in. If he lasted through the night it would be amazing, I tried to tell myself. Nuts. I was still plenty worried about Jo-Anne by the time the BMT let me off a couple of blocks from Barrett's office.

"Sit down, Chase," Tad Barrett told me a few minutes later. "There's a family resemblance, all right." I looked at him and liked what I saw. Clean-cut and tweedy, a pipe smoker with everything from meerschaum to yellow-boles on the rack in front of him. And big enough to start pushing people around if the going got tough. Now he tossed a pocket-sized book on the desk in front of him and grinned at me.

"A lot of us read Mike Hammer for kicks," he admitted. "Here's a secret, Chase: it's more fantastic than science-fiction. What can I do for you?"

"It's a long story," I said.

"Go ahead and bend my ear. That's why the shingle's up outside."

"It goes on Ken's bill. I don't have spare cash, at the moment."

"Your brother's money is good. So far I haven't been able to do a thing for him."

I thought that was peculiar but let it pass. If I'd had no trouble with Wompler, Barrett should have had even less. I told Barrett about Dr. Kincaid and his forthcoming book while he broke open a can of Mixture 79 and fired one of his pipes. I gave him everything: how Jo-Anne had pulled her practical joke, how we'd found

Phyllis Kirk last night, how Phyllis had written Wilson Wompler's business number down some time before she was murdered, how Jo-Anne had been sent to live with the Kincaids under guard but had slipped away and was probably prowling around through the snow somewhere right now.

"That's what has me worried," I said. "Whoever took the Kincaid papers will realize they're useless unless he can break the code. So Jo-Anne might be walking right into his arms."

Barrett emptied ash from his pipe into a large bronze tray and frowned at me. "These papers, Chase. Are they everything you say?"

"You figure it. Five hundred people, many of them rich and important, answer all sorts of personal questions. Some of the questions might send the wife packing to Reno, others might bring down the Internal Revenue boys or the Better Business Bureau or even the F.B.I."

"Do the police know this?"

"If they talked to Dr. Kincaid, they know."

"Then you want me to find the Stedman girl, is that it?"

I shrugged. "Break the whole thing if you can do it. I'll look for Jo-Anne myself. If you can find the guy who took the papers and killed Phyllis Kirk, no one's going to hurt Jo-Anne. I've got one other safeguard, too."

"What is it?"

"Me," I said. "A clay pigeon. I let Wompler think I can break the Kincaid code. Of course, it's not true. Only Kincaid and Jo-Anne know the code. But if Wompler's mixed up in this thing, let him go gunning for me instead of Jo-Anne."

"You're all right, Chase," Barrett said. "That takes guts."

I sat there staring at Barrett and wondering. When I'd mentioned Wilson Wompler the first time, it didn't get a rise out of him. But if Barrett had been after Wompler on that blackmail business, the coincidence should have struck him at once. He acted as if he didn't even know who Wompler was.

"I wish I could give you more to work with," I said. "If anything comes up, I'll let you know."

"I'll keep in touch with you," Barrett said. "Where can I reach you?"

"I don't know about tonight." There was a lot I still had to do. "But starting tomorrow, my brother's place. You have the number?"

Barrett nodded, we shook hands, and I asked if I could use his phone. A moment later I was speaking to Dr. Kincaid again. Jo-Anne hadn't been heard from, but the cops had issued an all-points bulletin for her. Phyllis Kirk's family, I learned, lived in Forest Hills. It was snowing so hard up in Putnam County, Jo-Anne couldn't return there even if she wanted to, except by train. Then she'd disappeared in a car? Yes, a '49 Dodge convertible. No skid chains or winter tires. The State Police had checked the Taconic Parkway all the way down to Hawthorne Circle, though, and she wasn't stuck on it. I thanked Dr. Kincaid for the information and called Guido to take him up on that beer. He had a little information, but not much. It could keep. I'd meet him tonight at nine in a bar on Eighth Avenue.

Barrett was picking up the phone himself when I left. "Calling the Credit Bureau," he explained. "To start a file on this Wompler guy."

* * * *

Chase Construction and Management Corporation had erected a few apartment buildings in Forest Hills, but we hadn't been able to compete with the two outfits which almost monopolized the long curving stretch of Yellowstone Boulevard and the fertile cliff-dweller territory to north and south. The snow had been falling harder out here, a dozen miles from the heart of the city. My damp feet had been warmed by the subway but began freezing again as soon as I stepped out into the night.

The Kirks lived in one of those six-story jobs set far back from the street, with a snow-mantled garden in front and a fair-to-middling lobby done in colonial furniture because the building was named after one of America's early presidents. I leaned against the downstairs bell and was rewarded with an answering buzz immediately, as if the Kirks craved company.

It was apartment 5-F. Mrs. Kirk came to the door wearing black and no make-up. Here eyes were swollen and red-rimmed. Behind her I could hear a low, sad murmur of conversation and caught a glimpse of many people in the living room.

"I'm a friend of Phyllis' roommate," I said, as gently as I could. "I'd like to talk with you, Mrs. Kirk."

"Is it very cold out, Mr....?"

"Jason Chase, ma'am. It's cold."

"My poor girl. We're burying her tomorrow, you know. Out there, in all that snow, in all that cold."

"There, Millie." It must have been her husband, joining us now. "There, Millie. The gentleman came to pay his respects."

"That was silly of me," Mrs. Kirk said, although her tone hadn't changed. She was beyond crying, and hurting all the more inside. "But she was so young," she said. "Why should anyone want to kill our Phyllis?"

"It was a terrible tragedy," I said. I tried to keep my voice soft but I suspected it was heard by all those mourners sitting around listlessly inside. "I wouldn't like to see it happen again to another young girl."

"Come in, Mr. Chase," Mrs. Kirk said and led me toward the living room.

"Make it the kitchen," I said. "It won't take long."

So, we were seated around the kitchen table and I went on, "Jo-Anne is in trouble. The same thing."

"Jo-Anne's a nice girl," said Mrs. Kirk.

"What do you mean, Chase?" Kirk asked me.

"She's on the prowl for your daughter's killer. I know the cops want him and will get him eventually, but Jo-Anne is like that. If you can give me some indication of—"

"Just a minute, young man," Mr. Kirk said. "You just missed Jo-Anne by about an hour. She was here."

"Oh, no."

Kirk nodded. "Paid her respects, asked some questions. You know."

"What kind of questions?"

"Paid her respects and stopped in out of the cold a while," Mrs. Kirk said.

"What did she ask you? Please try and remember."

"Well, now," Mrs. Kirk said. "Let me see..."

"Mainly, she wanted to know if our Phyllis ever talked about the Kincaid research," Kirk told me.

"You know," said Mrs. Kirk, "just questions while she warmed up."

"Did she ever talk about it?" I asked.

"Some," Kirk said. "We told Jo-Anne that a publisher called her a few days ago. He got our number from the Dean of Faculty at Columbia, I guess. They didn't know Phyllis and Jo-Anne were living in that bachelor-girl apartment."

"It was such a pretty place," Mrs. Kirk said.

"What was the publisher's name," I demanded, "Wompler?"

"Yes. Yes, that was it. Wompler. Funny you should know."

I said, "Did you tell Jo-Anne?"

Kirk nodded. "As a matter of fact, we did. Is anything the matter?"

An eight-year-old boy wandered into the kitchen for a glass of water. "Mama," he said, "When's Phyllis coming home? It's cold out."

"Norman," Kirk said.

"We had them so far apart," Mrs. Kirk told me. "He's still a baby. He's all we've got."

"I on'y wanted to know," Norman pleaded.

"You go back inside and play with your cousins," Mrs. Kirk said.

"Did she ask anything else, Mr. Kirk?"

"No, that was about it. It was all we could tell her. Is she in some kind of trouble?"

"I don't know," I told them truthfully. "I've got to find her. You've been a big help. You've been swell." I shook hands with Mr. Kirk and nodded to his wife. "I'm sorry about this," I said, and watched Mrs. Kirk swallow with difficulty. As I reached the front door, it was quiet in the living room. Half the people there were huddled over crossword puzzles, their pencils darting down nervously to scribble a word every time they thought of something. They avoided one another's eyes desperately, as if looking at each other would tighten the common bond of tragedy and make them all cry at once.

CHAPTER EIGHT

An hour later, I picked up Guido Isaac in the Club Enchantment on Eighth Avenue. It was neither a club nor very enchanting but it was good for a beer and I had a bottle of Blatz while Guido kept swatting me on the back with a bony hand and saying, "It's you. It's really you. Man, you can wallop like a mule. I ain't forgot it, Jason."

"Sure," I said. I swallowed the last of the beer and looked at my watch. Almost nine-thirty. "What did you find out about Wompler?"

He shrugged expressively and scratched at kinky hair. "Not much, I guess. Five years ago he got in trouble for peddling pornographic comic books, but got off with a stiff fine and a suspended sentence. I brung one of the books if you want to see."

I shook my head. "I've got to get going, Guido."

"The same business?"

"Wompler."

"I got nothing to do. I can tag along."

"Why get yourself involved?" I said.

"Because you got yourself involved with me."

"I don't think you ought to."

"Trouble?"

"I don't know. Maybe."

"Deal me in," Guido said cheerfully, finishing his own beer. "Lookit this." He lifted his jacket and revealed the butt of an automatic in his belt.

"Keep that thing out of sight," I grunted. "You want to go back up?"

"I thought you might be able to use it."

I considered this and said, "Okay. Give."

"Nope. She goes with me. Am I dealt, Jason?"

I grinned at him. "Guido, there's something about you. You're dealt."

He buttoned a frayed tweed coat up to his neck while I paid for our beers. "Your man Wompler lives over in the East Side in Peter Cooper."

A cold wind knifed across Manhattan from the Hudson, shrinking the snowflakes and drying them so they stung your face like needles. Traffic was snarled in the snow on Eighth Avenue, the horns arguing all up and down the street. It took us twenty minutes to find a cab and another half-hour to work our way across town past the stalled cars and angry drivers with all sorts of interesting appointments to keep.

At ten-thirty we stood outside Wilson Wompler's apartment in Peter Cooper Village, Guido thumping his hands together to warm them. I leaned on the bell and kept on leaning while Guido was stamping the last of the slush from his shoes.

The door opened and Wompler's fiercest scowl peeked out of the top of a voluminous woolen bathrobe. It failed to frighten me. "Just what kind of damn big wheel do you think you are?" he growled at me. "I have a good mind to…Jason Chase!"

"You have a good mind to what?"

"Well, you're the third person to bother me tonight."

"One was Jo-Anne Stedman," I told him. "Who was the other?"

I moved into the apartment, followed by Guido. Wompler grumbled and preceded us into the living room, flicking a light switch as he went. The furnishing was ultra-functional, with butterfly chairs casting big, birdlike shadows on the stark white walls, and the semi-lewd abstractions hanging there and doing fantastic things to the female figure. Before we could settle ourselves in the butterfly chairs, Audrey came padding into the living room from the hallway to our left. She wore her blonde hair loose around her sleek shoulders and satin lounging pajamas were draped straight and shimmering from her high pointed breasts. She didn't look sleepy. Inside somewhere I could hear soft music playing. It didn't take much to figure out what we had interrupted.

"That's true," Wompler said. "Miss Stedman was here asking about how I knew Phyllis Kirk. She wasn't the only one."

"I'm listening," I said.

"Why are you getting all hot and bothered about this thing, anyhow?"

I shrugged out of my coat, which Audrey took. She got behind Guido, towering over him, and helped him out of his overcoat. She padded barefoot back into the hall and hung both garments in a closet.

"I only want to know what happened to Jo-Anne," I said. "Where did she go?"

"All you people think I've got something to do with these Kincaid papers. I wouldn't lie to you, Chase. I'm clean. Why should I..."

"You already told me why. Phyllis Kirk was going to do an article for *Hush*. You liked the idea."

"But she's dead. It looks like I won't get my article after all."

"What did Jo-Anne want?"

"I told you. I explained how Miss Kirk had wanted to do an article for my magazine. She said she found it hard to believe."

"Why?"

"Because she didn't think Miss Kirk would have broken her trust like that. I shrugged and said that's what happened, just like I told her."

"It's the truth," said Li'l Audrey, bobbing her blonde head up and down. "I was right here." She winked at me. "Right here in Grand Central Station, I might add."

"Who else paid you a visit?"

"A private operative from the Tad Barrett Detective Agency," Wompler said, smoothing his wavy brown hair into place. "He said you hired Barrett to find the missing Kincaid papers. But it looks like you're throwing your money away if you go dogging the eye's footsteps."

"Maybe," I said. "Then what did Jo-Anne do?"

"She left with the detective. She said she wanted to see this Barrett. She said they were after the same thing, and maybe could help each other." Wompler grinned ruefully. "Have a heart and call it a night, Chase. It's late."

"How long ago was Jo-Anne here?"

Wompler asked Audrey for the time and she barefooted into the hall again. She was an amazing creature, that girl. There was so much of her, six feet and probably a hundred and fifty pounds, but all of it was miraculously in place and the lounging pajamas did things for the muscles, smoothing them into curves.

"It's a quarter to eleven, Willie."

"Then she was here an hour and a half ago," Wompler told me.

I nodded. "I hope you're telling the truth, Wompler. This means a lot to me and I don't want to find out you're lying."

"He has nothing to hide from you or anybody," Audrey said. She stood in front of Wompler almost protectively, her arms crossed just below her breasts, cushioning them. "And let me tell you something else, Mr. Chase. I try to act like a lady, but sometimes people don't let me. This is the second time you called Willie a liar today. I told you, his blood pressure."

"I didn't call him anything. I said I hoped he was telling the truth. Can I use your phone, Wompler?"

"Help yourself. It's in the hall."

I found the phone, one of those new jobs with the numbers outside the little holes, and dialed information for Tad Barrett's home address. He caught it midway through the second buzz, so probably I wasn't disturbing anything over there. "This is Jason Chase," I said. "Sorry to bother you so late, but something's come up."

"I'm having a nightcap, Chase. Go ahead."

"Has Jo-Anne Stedman been over to see you tonight?"

"Stedman? Oh, the dead girl's roommate. No. No, she hasn't. Should she have?"

"Did one of your operatives visit Wilson Wompler at home tonight?"

"As a matter of fact, yes. He reported in by phone and said he hadn't learned much."

"Did he say anything about Jo-Anne?"

"He didn't mention her at all. Is anything wrong, Chase?"

I said I didn't know and hung up.

"Now that he's confirmed everything," Wompler suggested, "why don't you go on home?"

"Jo-Anne never saw him. His operative didn't say anything about meeting Jo-Anne here."

"That's crazy, Chase. Maybe he didn't understand you."

"Maybe *you* don't. I said this was important."

"Then Barrett is lying," Audrey said. "I was right here. I saw the girl leave with Barrett's detective."

"Maybe this dick didn't tell his boss. Maybe he has an angle of his own," Wompler said.

Why would Wompler and the girl want to lie about Jo-Anne? I couldn't figure it out; but that they were lying, I was sure.

I was on Jo-Anne's trail all right, but not getting anywhere. The more I thought about it, the more I was willing to wring necks to find the answer. Wompler's neck or Li'l Audrey's, I wasn't particular.

"Hey, Guido," I said. "You keep an eye on Audrey here. Wompler and I are going inside to have a little talk."

Audrey shook her blonde head. "He stays with me." But Guido was suddenly pointing his .38 at her and waving her off into the far corner of the room with it. "Please do like he says, lady, and there won't be no trouble." He'd never pass Grammar One, but he got the point across and confirmed it by planting himself in front of her. You could see Audrey's face, chin and all, above his head.

"We'll try the bedroom," I told Wompler. "I'm in no hurry at all, but I want the truth out of you. Now move." He walked ahead of me out of the room, muttering how he was telling the truth and I'd never get away with this. As it turned out, his second statement was a hundred percent correct.

I heard Guido shout, "Hey!" I whirled back to see what was going on in the living room.

Li'l Audrey had forgotten she was a lady. I turned in time to see her uncork a right-handed uppercut which would have done a lot of men proud. It connected flush with Guido's jaw and sent him staggering across the room, crashing into a cocktail table and landing on his back on the floor. He scrambled to his feet, still holding the gun, but then flopped down to hands and knees again. I just stood there, trying to shut my mouth. Audrey got hold of his tie with her left hand, jerking him erect. The knuckles of her right fist almost scraped the floor as she brought it up again and there was a loud click which said Guido would have to pay his dentist a visit in the near future. When Audrey let go of his tie, Guido lay there, leaking blood from his mouth to the carpet.

Ex-lady grappler! She should have tried boxing. She had Guido's gun, too.

I thought she'd start hollering at me and I was ready for anything, but she stood there panting, staring not at me, not at Guido, but at Wompler. She tried to say something and got all choked up over it, then she began to cry. I caught the words, "...to act like a lady...you never let me...always mixed up in something like this...didn't want to hit him, but...going to hurt you...Willie, Willie..."

I walked to her and she didn't try to stop me when I unwrapped her long fingers from Guido's gun. I went into the kitchen for a glass of water and sloshed it on Guido's face. He spluttered and blinked and staggered upright holding a jaw which was already beginning to swell.

I looked at Audrey and figured she'd make more noise next time and maybe do more damage now that she knew Guido wouldn't use the gun.

"Oh, God," Wompler pleaded, "Get out of here. This is a bachelor apartment. I've got a reputation to maintain."

"If you're lying about Jo-Anne, I'll get you for it."

"Honest, Chase. Honest. It's the truth. Just get out of here. Honest."

So I supported Guido over to the closet and helped him on with his coat. "If anything happens to her, I'll kill you," I said.

"Honest," Wompler said. "Honest, Chase."

Guido still needed my support outside on the street. It was snowing harder.

We found a luncheonette still open on Second Avenue, and I bought Guido a cup of coffee and told him I was sorry.

"You should be sorry? It was all my fault. I fouled up on you. Letting a dame push me around like that."

"She used to wrestle professionally."

"I'll make it up to you, Jason. Just give me another chance, that's all. Listen, Jason. I'm working now in a used-car lot up in the Bronx. You want anything, anything at all, I'll help. I only ask you should let me try. I know my way around. I got connections. Only please don't think because of what happened I'm no good to you." The lower half of his face was red and puffy and you couldn't tell if he was smiling or scowling or what. But his eyes were pleading.

"Okay," I said. "That's a promise."

"My pal. I can still crack this thing for you."

"Listen. You get any ideas about it, don't do anything except call me. A promise for a promise."

"Sure, anything you say. I'll call you."

"My brother's place on Park Avenue." I gave Guido the number and paid our check. We went outside together and I watched Guido disappear into the night, a small, slumping figure of a man who compensated inside for what he lacked in stature.

Then I caught the bus uptown and grinned for no reason at all, except that I realized I hadn't disturbed my last household yet tonight. Only Ken wouldn't mind.

And Julia would be delighted.

CHAPTER NINE

Neither Ken nor Julia answered the door. Stephanie did.

I stared. She didn't really look like Julia. She looked like what I'd always wanted in Julia. She was a younger, idealized version of the same girl, but there were subtle differences in the way she stood, in the frankness of her eyes and voice, in the completely genuine smile that parted her lips and lit up her whole face.

"Jason," she said. "This is a wonderful surprise."

"What are you doing here?"

"Now, don't get upset. It's because of what happened. Maybe you shouldn't have said what you said, but Pop was to blame mostly. I let him know that's what I thought, and here I am."

"What about Emma? She didn't let you go, did she?"

"Pop didn't either. I just packed a bag and walked out. I'm not saying it's permanent or anything, but I've got to let him cool off. I'm not running away or anything dramatic like that. It's why I came here to Julia's house. Now, what about you?"

"They invited me to stay until I got squared away."

"Well, get out of that wet coat. And there's still snow in your hair, enough to comb out and make a snowball with. Come on, get yourself dried out. I'm having cake and milk in the kitchen. If you can thaw out by midnight, I'll wait for you."

I made it with plenty of time to spare, but I must have splashed around too noisily in the bathroom, because when I walked into the kitchen a gathering of the clan was waiting for me.

"Jason, boy. I'm glad you're here. Got plenty of room for both you and Steffy. Bring some cheer into the gloomy Chase household, eh, Julia?" He chuckled and caught Julia's cheek playfully between thumb and forefinger. She smiled mechanically.

They remained with us for a while, chatting idly about nothing in particular. At last they headed into the foyer, each going a different direction in the long hall. So Ken and Julia maintained separate bedrooms! Julia's words that morning came back to me and I couldn't help feeling sorry for her. Then I forgot all about her and gazed at her beautiful younger sister.

"Please, Jason. You'll make me blush."

"I can't help it. I'd like to spend a lot more time looking at you."

"Jason."

"No, really."

"Please stop."

"All right," I said. "You never did tell me what you hoped to accomplish at Wompler's."

"The same as you did. Incidentally, it didn't work out."

"What didn't work out?"

"Wompler must have changed his mind again. When I asked Julia about it tonight she said Ken had called Wompler and he refused to give up the prints."

"What the hell! That doesn't make sense."

"That's what she said. So it looks like I'm still in business up there."

"That no good son has been lying his fool head off to me. Every time he opens his mouth, practically. I...I wish you'd forget about it anyway, Steffy."

"I can't. It's for Julia. If you're worrying about me, thanks, but you don't have to. I've got a friend up there who'll look out for me. Maybe you know her, that lady grappler, Audrey? She likes me and says if I ever have any trouble, just come to her."

"But what can you do about the blackmail?"

Stephanie rolled her eyes and then laughed. "Well, I'm a woman, Jason. Wompler's maybe kind of little, but he's male."

"Listen," I said, plunking my milk glass on the table and standing up. "If I even thought that dapper little liar was touching you, I'd..."

"Shh, you're shouting. You're sweet, Jason. But you don't have to worry about that, either. A girl can get a lot more results if she keeps her distance but sort of, well... Oh, I don't like to do such things, but I can't sit around while blackmail ruins Julia's marriage."

"You think that's what's ruining her marriage?"

"She thinks so."

"I got you into trouble with your father. Now I'm trying to even the score and get you out of some. No matter what happens with Wompler, this marriage is on the rocks."

"That's a spiteful thing to say. I know you're carrying a torch, but…"

"You've got it wrong, kid. I feel nothing for Julia now. I thought she was someone but it turned out she was someone else—I had this idea inside my head which the girl outside didn't fit. So it isn't that. I can't see you sticking your neck out over something which is going to pan out wrong no matter what you do, that's all."

"It's my neck, Jason. Please let's not talk about it."

"Well, it looks like all I do these days is try to keep girls I know out of trouble. So far I'm batting zero."

"Anything I can do?"

"No. Good night."

After she'd gone, I sat on the Chinese Modern sofa and had a couple of shots of Canadian. I was worrying about Jo-Anne, worrying good and hard. But deep down, I remained aware of Stephanie. What was there about that kid? I walked back to the kitchen. The faint fragrance of her was there, still lingering like an unfelt kiss in the air.

I decided on sleep and walked down the foyer to my room. "Jason Chase," I said, thinking the words and then realizing I was saying them out loud, "You're falling in love with the girl."

I shut the door and found a pair of Ken's pajamas on the bed. I fell asleep thinking of Jo-Anne—and Stephanie.

* * * *

Suddenly I sat up in bed. It seemed to me that the door had opened and shut, waking me.

"What the hell do you want?" I said.

There came the soft sound of footsteps on the carpet.

Ken? What the devil was he after at this hour?

"Damn it, Ken. Get out of here."

"Shh! You'll wake them." A woman, whispering. "It's Steffy, silly."

The bed creaked. The mattress tilted sideways under her weight. I sat there, not moving, not thinking. I could see nothing in the blackness. I was wide awake and then the one thought was running through my head. Not Steffy. Please, not Steffy, not like this.

Her hand touched my shoulder. I sat still, I didn't want to move. She made a mewing sound, like a cat, and then she had lifted my hand to her lips and was kissing it.

"Steffy," I said. "Steffy?"

And then her arms around my neck and the warmth of her against my chest, curled there; and I could smell that perfume in her hair and maybe she could feel my heart pounding too and she mewed again when I lifted her face and opened her lips with mine and burned with her, on fire, and found room to mumble, "I love you, Steffy, I love you…"

And tasted the whisky on her lips.

"Julia," I said, shocked back to my senses. And I was suddenly glad, glad because it wasn't Stephanie. But here I was in my brother's house with my brother's wife.

"Goddammit, Julia," I said.

She got out of there and fled down the foyer without looking back at me. I suddenly smiled foolishly. And then I stopped smiling, locked the door, went back to bed and lay there, staring at the darkness and unable to go to sleep.

Damn her. She'd borrowed Stephanie's perfume for the occasion.

* * * *

I poked at the two sunnyside eggs and four strips of bacon on my plate. Ken's head was lost in the financial pages of the *New York Times* while Julia and Stephanie finished their own breakfasts and began clearing the dishes. I'd have to get out of here. It didn't much matter where I went. Anywhere but here.

"Ken," I said. "Steffy tells me things didn't work out with Wompler."

The newspaper folded. Ken made a bridge of his hands over his empty plate and asked, "How did Steffy find out?"

"I told her," Julia said.

Ken didn't look surprised. "Well, it was a good try, boy. Apparently you scared Wompler so he'd say anything to get you out of his hair. But as soon as you left, he changed his mind." He spoke about it matter-of-factly, as if an adulterous wife who was being blackmailed was the most natural topic of breakfast conversation in the world. It hardly seemed to bother Julia, either; she went right on clearing dishes. Stephanie had the grace to blush.

The phone rang.

Ken got up and picked the receiver off the wall-box extension. "Hello? Yes, Barrett... Oh, not about that, eh?... My brother? Yes, he's here. Just a minute. It's for you, Jason. Tad Barrett."

I took the receiver and said, "Jason Chase."

"Chase, I'm sorry. I've got tragic news."

"Jo-Anne?" I said.

"Yes. I'm sorry."

I gagged emptily on the sour taste of coffee. I didn't want to hear the rest of it. I fought a crazy impulse to hang up the phone. I swallowed and felt my heart hammering.

I said, "The worst?"

"The worst."

"God! How did..."My voice broke. Julia and Ken and Stephanie all were watching me.

"Take it easy, Chase. You'd better come down here." He gave me the address of a dock on South Street, which I scribbled mechanically on the wall pad hanging by the phone. My hand was trembling so much I had to lean against the pad to steady it.

"I'll be right down," I said. I hung up.

Stephanie spoke. "What is it, Jason?"

"Why don't you just shut up and leave me alone, all of you? I shouldn't have been here in bed last night while..." My voice broke again.

"Jason. Can I help?"

"Nothing can help. Jo-Anne is dead." I stood there and bawled. I just bawled like a baby. Then I honked my nose and found Stephanie waiting with a bottle of Canadian. I didn't look for a glass but tilted the bottle to my lips and kept pulling and pulling.

They knew Jo-Anne. She'd been one of our crowd since I had met her at school.

I said, "I'm going to find the bastard who did it and kill him slow."

Stephanie stood in the doorway and said, "You'd better not go out like that."

I smiled at her. A real smile. I got my hands under her arms and lifted her out of the way, depositing her alongside the door.

Outside, the big snow-sweepers were eating up great steel mouthfuls and spraying them up on the Park Avenue mall. I saw a cab letting off passengers at a hotel a block away. I sprinted for it and said, "South Street."

CHAPTER TEN

It was nine-thirty when I got there. The hack had had a rough time with the fish-market carts being pushed and dragged across the street and up the street and down the street, loaded with crates of cod and mackerel and maybe sea serpent, for all I knew, all completely ignoring the traffic.

The dock-hands wore mackinaws or leather jackets with baling hooks slung across the shoulders. I got out and maneuvered along the sidewalks stacked solid with crates and barrels, behind which you could see the open fronts of the great downtown fish markets, where naked electric bulbs hung over the stalls of fish and seafood and tried to dispel the gloom under the spanking new expressway which carried traffic overhead.

The cold air reeked of fish as I pushed on, coming to a small dock beyond the last of the stalls, jutting into the river between them and the Coast Guard Station. The police photographic crew was just leaving when I got there, loading their gear into the big weatherproof cases.

"You see all kinds," one of the boys was saying.

"Yeah, but not like this right after breakfast. They'd of told me, I wouldn't of had that extra cruller." He made a face. "I'm gonna be in no hurry to get these shots in the hypo, no sir."

I walked by. The crowd was ten deep and trying to push closer to the dock. I shouldered my way through and some voices started to protest, but when they looked at my face they changed their minds and gave me all the room I wanted.

The cop standing at the foot of the dock didn't. "You can't go any further, buddy," he said.

"She has no family. I'm her closest friend. I can identify her."

"Then you must be Jason Chase."

"That's right."

"A private detective out on the dock told the Lieutenant about you, Mr. Chase. It's all right for you to go on up there." The cop stamped his feet to keep them warm and waved me on.

The dock sagged and creaked underfoot. There were rot-holes through which you could glimpse the dirty gray water and the barnacle-encrusted pilings.

Tad Barrett came trotting across the rotten wood toward me. A big briar hung slackly from his teeth and he wasn't smiling. "It isn't pretty, Chase. A time like this, a man wishes he could say something."

"Let's take a look," I said.

The uniformed police were thick as flies. The plain-clothesmen walked about briskly and efficiently, hopping on and off a big but ancient cruiser which was slapping back and forth against the pilings with the tidewater.

"Down there." Barrett pointed. "On the boat. A contact I have on Homicide Squad, Manhattan West, tipped me off."

It was old and weathered, that boat, and looked like something out of those B-movies about steamers which ply the Belgian Congo in search of trouble and exotic romance.

Two plainclothesmen nodded curtly at Barrett and I recognized one of them. He'd been with Pop Grujdzak that night when Phyllis Kirk was murdered. Barrett jerked a finger toward the boat's cabin, gave one of the cops a questioning look and waited until the man nodded. We stepped down and through a beaten-up bulkhead.

Someone had got a kerosene lamp going inside. You could smell it and had to adjust your eyes to its flickering light.

Pop Grujdzak rasped out of the shadows, "You seem to have a nose for murder, Chase."

"Can it," I said. "Where is she?"

Pop pointed. The cops had draped the body with a tarpaulin and I almost didn't want to look, but I picked up the kerosene lamp by its handle and squatted near the tarp, lifting a corner.

They'd worked over Jo-Anne's face with a baling hook or something. There were bloodstains on her clothing and the way she lay there indicated some of her bones had been broken. I was glad I'd done my bawling in Ken's apartment, but I had to turn away and shut my eyes tight and stand off in a shadowy corner of the cabin for a while. They were still talking, the cops. Two men whispering. Pop Grujdzak's rasp. You could hear the water slapping against the pilings outside. I turned around and looked at Barrett, who had placed the kerosene lamp back on its tin bracket.

"Who did it?" I said.

"We don't know yet."

"How did it happen?"

"From what Lieutenant Grujdzak tells me, it happened like this. Someone took her here. Two men, maybe three. They worked her over pretty bad…"

"To get the code out of her!"

"They were going to dump her in the river. See, over there, that pail of bricks? They'd have anchored her with that and it might have been a long time before the body washed up any place, if at all."

"But they didn't."

"No, they didn't. The Lieutenant tells me a patrolman on the beat last night spotted the light here and heard what sounded like a woman sobbing. He came running and got knocked down for his trouble. He thought there were two men, but there might have been three, he says. He fired twice and missed them in the darkness. Then he went back and found Miss Stedman."

"What killed her, Barrett?"

"Loss of blood. Shock. A crushed trachea. The medical report hasn't been made yet, but when the patrolman found her, she was still alive. She died before the ambulance got here, which was two o'clock this morning."

"And they made her suffer?"

"Yeah," Barrett said, "they made her suffer. Hell, look at her."

I didn't. I said, "I'm going to get those bastards, Barrett." I was whispering. I hoped the cops wouldn't hear. I hoped mostly Pop Grujdzak wouldn't hear. I was an ex-con and they wouldn't have too much trouble slapping me in jail on one pretext or another. "I don't want the cops to get them, Barrett. The law's too soft and moves too slow and kills too quick. I want to find them. Me. I want to get them."

"Were you in love with the poor kid, Chase?"

"I'd have done anything for her. Anything. No, I wasn't in love with her. That's the worst part of it. She was the best, Barrett. The best there is. It just wasn't there."

"About what you said, Chase, I sympathize with you. But hell, man, you ought to cool off. You ought to tell the cops what you know and let them take it from there. Two people have been murdered over this thing already."

"Like hell," I said. "I don't want the cops to find those guys. I'm going to prowl around and keep on prowling till I find something, if it takes the rest of my life. If the cops get close, I'll try to keep them off the trail. I want those people. Two or three or a hundred, I don't care. I'm going to get them."

"What do you mean, you'll prowl around? How do you conduct a murder investigation, Chase? Do you know anything about it? You'd be batting your head against a stone wall."

"Then you help me," I said. "Stay on the case and let me work with you."

"The cops don't like one-man vendettas."

"Then nuts to the cops. I'm going to get them, that's all. Who owns this derelict?"

"Don't yell. It's Wilson Wompler."

"What!"

"Yeah, Wompler. He bought it for a few hundred a couple of weeks ago, according to what I could find out. Going to shoot a picture story on white slavery or some such fool thing, and this was to be the scenery."

"Then that means…"

"It doesn't mean a thing, not necessarily."

"Has anyone talked to Wompler about it?"

"Not me. The police have, though."

"What did he say?"

Barrett shrugged. "They didn't tell me. They don't tell me everything."

"Are you staying with the case?"

Barrett was still shrugging. "I don't see why not. You hired me to find a killer, and maybe the missing Kincaid papers. Sure I'm staying with the case."

"I appreciate that. Maybe in a day or so I'll be coming to you saying I don't know which way to turn."

"We'll give you all the cooperation we can, Chase."

"*We* won't." It was Pop Grujdzak's rasp. I had no way of knowing how much he had heard, but whatever it was it was too much.

"The police don't tell you Chase boys how to run your construction business, so we don't want you horning in on our murders."

"The cops told us how to run it. They sent me to jail."

"I'll spell it out for you, Chase. I don't care what happens to you. I don't care if you get run over by a steamroller tomorrow. But when you monkey in police business and then get hurt, that I don't like. Maybe if Miss Stedman didn't go poking her nose into murder, she'd still be alive."

"Yeah? And maybe if your cops were able to keep her up in Putnam County like they were supposed to, she'd still be alive."

"They were there to keep trouble away from her, not keep her away from trouble."

"It's the same thing. They lost her."

"She was like Lot's wife. That they couldn't help."

I cursed to stop from poking him one. Emma had been right. When he was whipped back into a corner, he used the Bible for a shield. You couldn't tell what, if anything, he really believed in.

Barrett and I got out on deck and climbed back to the dock. "Good luck, Chase," he said. "And keep in touch."

I promised I would and headed uptown to Wompler Publications.

* * * *

"Really, Chase. I have an appointment in ten minutes. This whole nasty business is playing hob with my schedule."

"Sit down," I said. I poked Wompler back into his chair. He started to bound up again, then changed his mind as he looked at me.

"His blood pressure," Audrey warned.

I'd barged right by sets One through Five, not even bothering to see if Stephanie had reported for work. Wompler was dressed in a pin-stripe suit and Audrey was undressed in halter and shorts as if she'd just come off the set.

"I want to ask you some questions," I told Wompler.

"I said I'm busy."

Audrey moved between us. "I'll have to ask you to leave, Mr. Chase."

I wasn't playing games, with her or anyone else. I made a lewd gesture which told her what I thought of her suggestion. Apparently she forgot how much she wanted to be a lady. What she'd done to little Guido had probably gone to her blonde head. She started to swing at me.

I caught her balled fist in my hand and twisted. She yelped and followed it around, spinning away from me. I yanked the fist up, then shoved, and she took two staggering steps toward Wompler and sprawled across his lap. She glared up at me and whined, "Fighting a lady. Aren't you brave?"

"It's all different now," I said. "You can forget that lady crap. If you get in the way, I'll kick your teeth in, and that's a promise."

She looked at me. Subdued, but seething.

"I heard the cops were here," I told Wompler.

"About the other girl, yes. That's a shame, Chase."

"What did you tell them?"

"Why should I have to tell them anything?"

"Because it was your boat, that's why."

"Ask Audrey where I was last night. Ask yourself, Chase. You saw us together."

"At ten-thirty."

"All night. Ask Audrey."

"As far as I know, you were the last one to see Jo-Anne alive. At your place, just before I got there."

"I told you she went off with the Barrett detective."

"Barrett denied it."

Audrey was still glaring at me, standing behind Wompler's chair. Now Wompler was glaring too. He had no comment to make about Barrett, so I said, "Do the police know of her visit?"

"No."

"How does this sound?" I asked. "Last night you told Jo-Anne the papers were downtown somewhere. She met you, say, at a bar. You took her down to your boat because you figured there'd be no disturbances there. You had the Kincaid papers, but they were no good to you unless you could get Jo-Anne to reveal the code. So you and Audrey tried to make her talk, then got scared and killed her. Maybe she talked and maybe she didn't, but a patrolman came along and scared you away before you had time to dispose of her."

Wompler's face had drained white. His throat worked, but it was some time before he could talk. Then his face got all red and he was shouting. "You're crazy," he cried. "You're a crazy, no good, meddling louse who has a mad on for me, I don't know why. I'm clean. I have nothing to do with this. If you don't stop-bothering me I'm going to call the cops, so help me."

"Go ahead and call them. But they don't know you were the last person to see her alive. They don't know yet."

"Oh, God," Wompler moaned. Audrey just stood there, nursing her forearm and not saying anything.

"Listen, Wompler. You shape up as a dirty liar every time you open your mouth. Maybe you're afraid of something and trying to cover, or maybe it's a disease with you. I don't know. But…"

"I'm asking you, Mr. Chase. Please. I'm a publisher. Some people say smut and smear, but I want to go classy. I had enough of that pervert stuff. All I want to do is mind my own business and publish good picture magazines. There's no reason I should lie to you, no reason at all. There's no reason you should keep on bothering me like this."

I grabbed him off the chair by the lapels of his pinstripe jacket. "Get this straight," I growled in his face. "I intend to find out who killed Jo-Anne." His lower lip was trembling. His nostrils were flaring with every breath he took. "You better hope you're not involved," I said. "You damn well better!"

I let him fall. Audrey caught him and eased him to the floor, where she sat down and ran her long fingers through his wavy hair, cooing to him softly. What the hell, I thought suddenly. That big broad with muscles must be his mother-image.

"You can go to the cops," she called as I left. "We should care. We were together all night."

I checked with the girls on the sets and found that Stephanie hadn't come in to work yet, which wasn't odd since most of them only put in one or two hours a day, then trotted their cheesecakes and cookies on home. A gent carrying a portfolio was out in the reception room, but I told him I didn't think Wompler would be seeing anyone for a while.

I needed a drink. I needed a whole passel of drinks.

But first I'd see if Guido could make like an armory and equip me for whatever my snooping might uncover.

Chapter Eleven

I found him at a used-car lot on Bruckner Boulevard in the Bronx, wiping snow from the automobile bargains with a plastic scraper. The boss was drinking coffee in the shed nearby, Guido said. The boss must have been not only of the old school but its president emeritus, for all the time we talked Guido pretended he was conning a potential buyer.

"How about this Chevy?" he said, and "Yeah, I can get you an equalizer. I ask you, ever see anything like it? 1946 model and only forty-seven thousand miles."

"It looks like a real beauty. I was hoping you could have it for me some time today."

"I'll try. Don't like the Chevys, huh?"

"I was looking for something with class. A pre-war Caddy or something, but cheap. If you can get hold of a sap too, I'd be much obliged."

"Have you found something, Jason?"

"Not yet."

"Well, you can leave it to Guido. I get through here this afternoon, I'm gonna go downtown and keep listening. I'll get the rumble for you. Reach you at the brother's place?"

"No, better not." Thanks to Julia, I wouldn't go back there. "You have any messages, call this private detective, Tad Barrett. Don't forget, I'm relying on you for the artillery."

Guido nodded, then put on his salesman's smile again as the owner of the lot waddled out of his shack. "Why don't you have a cup of coffee, friend, and think it over?" he wanted to know.

"I want to shop around a little," I said.

* * * *

Forty minutes later, I was prowling the bars on Fifty-second Street. Anything but a bar or a cheap nightclub along that drag was there strictly by mistake and probably wouldn't last out the season. But I didn't want company and I didn't want to remember. I only wanted to get lost for a couple of hours, then start all over again. How would a professional go about it? I didn't have the faintest idea. I just knew that somewhere in this city of eight million people there was a killer who had killed twice for the Kincaid papers and would cheerfully try for three if he thought it would do him any good. I had to find him.

But first I had to stop remembering for a while. Remembering Jo-Anne.

I made a considerable dent in the bourbon reserves of three bars. Maybe I couldn't quite walk a straight line after that, but I was still thinking up a storm and getting nowhere. I switched to Calvert's the way the ads tell you, with no better results. I thought maybe if I got in touch with Doc Kincaid and asked him for a list of people who had answered his questions I'd be able to find out if the killer had broken his code. It seemed like a fine idea, but I wasn't buying any of that, either. It was the professional way to go about things and it might bring results in a month or two or twenty, but I didn't have the time. I'd drink myself into an alcoholic ward long before that.

But Tad Barrett might like the idea and might be able to do more about it with a whole staff of trained operatives.

Jason Chase, you are a genius. You must drink to this brilliant idea. You must. You will. But the barman shook his head.

"What do you mean, I've had enough?"

"I mean, I don't think you ought to take another. Not here."

"That's ridiculous, my good sir."

After enough of them, they had begun to taste like tea. I got up and staggered outside into the crisp cold air. My head was foggy and somewhere up there alongside the TV tower on the Empire State Building.

But by the time I walked to Barrett's, the head was clearing; and I was back to remembering.

Barrett was reading another pocket-sized mystery job with a lurid cover showing a female with incredible breasts being scared silly by a trenchcoated silhouette complete with sawed-off shotgun.

"Come in, Chase," he said. "What the devil happened to you?"

"I look that bad, huh?"

"Your breath smells worse."

"I was trying to forget, a little. Friend of mine call? A fellow by the name of Guido?"

"Right. He said something about having the stuff."

"When can I pick it up?"

"He said he had something else, too. Information. He thinks he knows who did the job on Miss Stedman."

"What!" I was standing up and shouting. I didn't know who they were. They were still nameless. But I could almost feel my hands around their throats.

"Take it easy," Barrett advised. "He wants you to meet him tonight, in Brooklyn. He says that's where they hang out. He wants you to pick him up at 8:30 tonight. A place called The House That Jack Built."

"I'll find it." I stood up and shook hands with Barrett. "Maybe I ought to take you along. But I want to go it alone. I've got reasons. Can you understand that?"

"Sure. But will the cops understand?"

Without answering I walked out. I wandered over to the mid-town Y.M.C.A. and got a room. I went back outside and bought a cheap razor, some soap, a toothbrush and toothpaste. I scrubbed and lathered and scrubbed some more. I took a shower as hot as I could stand it. I was trembling now not with fatigue but with anticipation. Guido had something. A lead.

A couple of hours of sleep did me more good than all the wonder drugs ever discovered, and a dinner of pot roast with all the trimmings at a restaurant across the street completed the cure. At 7:30 I found the subway and headed down south to Brooklyn.

* * * *

The House That Jack Built proclaimed itself with a blinking neon sign. First it said *The House* in yellow, then *That Jack Built* in red, then the whole business in blue, then all over again. It held down a corner near where Nostrand Avenue crosses Flatbush Avenue, a couple of blocks behind the campus of the big, free city college there. There was a *Bud* sign in the window and a second floor that was dark. I'd arrived a few minutes early but walked inside anyway. The place smelled of stale smoke and staler beer.

A juke box competed with two five-cent bowling machines to see which could make the most noise.

I found Guido waiting for me in back, where the booths curved around behind the U-shaped bar. I sat down across from him and smiled while he handed me a package wrapped with brown paper! "It's a .45," he said. "Sorry it hadda be so bulky, Jason, but it's all I could rustle up."

"That's fine," I told him.

"And a sap. Man, you should see it. Weighted perfect. You only have to go flip"—Guido turned his hand over on the table—"and she slaps around hard enough to crush an elephant's skull. You'll like it, Jason. Drink?"

I ordered a beer while Guido lined up a third empty Blatz bottle with two others on the table. There was an electric feeling inside me. It was tingling down to my fingertips and made me want to go fifteen rounds with the champion slugger of The House That Jack Built or any other place. "What else have you got?" I asked.

"All sorts of contacts, Jason. Guido's been around. You already heard up the river, huh?"

I'd heard.

"Talk," I said. I hunched forward and peered at him and tried to read something in his dark face. He was keyed up and tense himself, but not scared.

"Barrett tell you?" he wanted to know.

"He told me you thought you found them."

"They're tough guys from the old days, Jason. I knew them a little. Mean boys. It should be your pleasure never to have anything to do with them."

"I'll have plenty to do with them."

Guido shrugged. "I got you down here in Brooklyn because this is their hangout. Also a place over on Livonia Street. After you think about it a little maybe, you can go to the cops and tell them."

"You got any proof?"

"Only a rumble."

"So the cops are out. Look, you don't have to go into this with me. I wish you wouldn't. Just tell me who they are."

"One is Five O'Clock McGuire. The other is Puggie LaBetta from Bensonhurst."

"Okay," I said. "Now I know. You can blow, Guido."

"Who fingered the girl, I ain't sure. But Puggie can tell you. Or Five O'Clock."

"I don't know how to thank you, Guido."

"Me you don't have to thank. I ask around a little from friends, I get to hear things."

"Do they know you've been looking? Puggie and Five O'Clock?"

"You think I'm an amachoor?"

"Not you, Guido. I shouldn't even have asked. I owe you something for this. Any time you…"

"You don't owe me. I already told you. For my friend Jason it is a real pleasure." He sipped beer. "But listen. Please don't go over there. To Livonia Street. Sometimes Puggie and Five O'Clock come to this place. It's a new hangout for some of the old crowd, but down on Livonia Street they're at home. They could tap the sidewalk like cops do with nightsticks and the hoods would come running to help them from all over. Here at least some people will be neutral."

"But you said they hang out there."

"They do. They run a numbers game in a pool room. But the cops are going to raid there soon, I hear, so maybe they'll all start drifting over to The House That Jack Built for a place to stay. All the gunsels, Jason. Better not to start anything there or here. Better you should call the law."

"Just come on outside and point my nose in the direction of Livonia Street, will you?" I said.

Guido shrugged and must have told himself it was useless to argue. I took the check and paid for our drinks, then we went outside into Nostrand Avenue.

An electric bus rumbled by, blue sparks flashing on the wire above it in the darkness. Some of the college crowd had gathered for the evening in front of a luncheonette two stores down.

It was nine o'clock and very cold, with a wintery clearness in the air so the dark cars parked along the curb were gleaming black under the street lights. Snow was banked dark and dirty against the curb.

"You take the bus toward New York," Guido said.

I looked where he pointed. I turned back and started to say something. Behind him I saw a car wheel around the corner, a black job which looked like an Olds, and come cruising slowly along Nostrand Avenue. When it came abreast of us, the back window rolled down. There was a man in front driving, another in the rear.

Something poked out of the rolled-down back window as the car crawled by.

I dove for Guido, but he was yelling already and throwing himself toward the sidewalk. A sub-machine gun hammered and roared and I could see the bright angry muzzle-flashes. I spun slowly, as in a dream. I could see the slugs kicking off the brick wall behind us, and I felt the pavement slap up against my hands and dirty snow in my face.

The plate-glass window of The House That Jack Built exploded with a roar as loud as the sub-machine gun, then something struck my shoulder and scalded, flipping me over on my back like the kick of a mule. Guido screamed once and his face was a bloody, shapeless ruin.

The Olds' tires squeaked and skidded in the slush. Except for that, it was very quiet. I fumbled with the package Guido had given me and ripped it open, clawing inside for the .45.

I started pulling the trigger as the Olds' tires finally held and it lurched forward. I got to my knees and kept firing, the .45 bucking savagely in my hand. The Olds jumped as one of the rear tires blew, then skidded sideways fifty yards down the block and plowed into a parked car. I got up and started running but I could see the doors opening and the shadows of the men inside the Olds sprinting down the street. The .45 clicked in my hand, empty. The Olds was empty too.

My legs wanted to dance in all sorts of directions, but I made it back to The House That Jack Built, and Guido.

He was still lying there where he had fallen, one hand over his face as if he were trying to protect it. Some of the college kids had come over and a girl was whimpering softly. I looked at Guido's face and didn't even have to feel for his pulse.

"Hey, mister. You're hurt."

"Take your hands off me," I said. "I've got to get them."

"You better stay still. You're bleeding all over."

I staggered back down the block towards the Olds. Far off I could hear a siren shrieking shrilly, coming closer.

The Olds' front fender was crumpled against a hardtop convertible parked in front of a butcher shop. I looked inside again and found nothing. I banged the glove compartment open with the butt of the .45 and groped around. There was a map of New York City, a pair of gloves, a little billfold with a plastic window which displayed a registration card. The letters swam in front of my eyes. I tried to steady them and realized my hands were wet with blood, smudging the plastic window.

Footsteps pounded down the street. I had to take off after Puggie and Five O'Clock. They had been wise to Guido, after all.

My left shoulder was numb. I couldn't move the arm. I opened the door. I had to take the bus to Livonia Street.

Two men caught me as I tumbled out of the Olds. One of them began ripping the jacket away from my shoulder. The siren wailed on top of me. Then cops were all over the place.

Names were taken. I said I was guilty of rent gouging. I said it over and over again until they had eased me down to the sidewalk and rolled up someone's coat under my head. Then I passed out.

CHAPTER TWELVE

It was a large square room, the walls painted green, the windows high but closed now against the pelting, icy rain. I was aware of the rain first, rattling against the windows, then the moaning of the little man who lay across the room from me in the only other occupied bed. He was sleeping and moaning in his sleep and under the sheet you could see the hard outline of a plaster cast from his neck down.

After a while a nurse came in with a tray of fruit juice but noticed the little guy was asleep and started walking out again.

"What about the non-paying customers?" I said. I wasn't really feeling too bad. Only tired, with a dull ache in my left shoulder and a stiffness in my left arm.

She'd forgotten how to smile, professionally or otherwise. She said, "Well, I see seventeen is awake."

She walked toward the bed with the tray of fruit juice balanced on one hand. I thought she was going to give me a glass of the stuff, but at the last moment her skinny hand darted into a pocket of her nurse's whites and came up with a thermometer which was then driven between my lips.

"Seventeen would like to know exactly where he is," I said.

"Keep your mouth closed, please."

"Mole kmph ym."

"That's better." After a time, she plucked the thermometer from my mouth, held it up, studied it, and wrote something on the chart at the foot of my bed. "The doctor will be here shortly," she said, and left the glass of fruit juice on my bedstand.

I leaned over and sucked. Sour grapefruit stuff.

"Guido," I said out loud, quite suddenly. "God." And then it all came rushing back.

A white-smocked doctor entered the ward, nodded, squinted anxiously at my bandaged shoulder.

I obliged him with regular breathing when he applied a stethoscope to my chest. I coughed when he said cough. I looked at the ceiling while he examined the whites of my eyes.

"You are in the proverbial pink, Mr. Chase." He beamed. "Another week in bed and you'll be a new man."

"A week!" I roared. "I can't stay here a week."

"Oh, you must. It was a flesh wound, but you took a nasty fall. There's been a slight bone separation, you see. Between the humerus and the scapula. Be glad this isn't a private hospital, where they'd hang on to you ten days or two weeks. Here at Kings County, we don't have the bed space. Now, if you're feeling as strong as you look…"

"I feel like a million bucks, doc. I could get out of here right now."

"Hardly. However, if you're feeling that good, some men from Kings County Homicide have been waiting here to see you."

I sighed, while the doctor went to summon his fellow city employees. Kings County Homicide. At least it wouldn't be Pop Grujdzak.

All three of them wore civvies. Two were tall and hefty. The third was broad and red-headed. They commenced firing questions, the two tall men on either side of me, the fat one at the foot of the bed studying my medical history. "Did you see the men in the car?"

"What were you doing in Brooklyn at the time, Chase?"

"Where'd you get the .45?"

"It's a violation of the Sullivan Law, you realize?"

"You knew Guido Isaac in prison. Was this the result of some prison fight?"

"Funny how you and Guido should get together right after you got out!"

"What were you planning, Chase?"

"Cut out that crap!" I yelled. It got through their grease-gun tactics. They all shut up at once and I could hear the man across the room still moaning. I said, "If you're going to play that once-a-criminal-always-a-criminal routine with me, you know what you can do. I'll cooperate with you guys because we're all after the same thing, Guido's killer. But if you want it that way, I'll start hollering for a lawyer, and that's a promise."

"We didn't mean anything like that, Chase."

I did some fast thinking. Exactly how much should I tell the Kings County boys?

"Well," I said, "you probably know about the Stedman murder in New York."

"We know. We checked you and Guido with B.C.I. and your name popped up in the Stedman case. Had a long talk with Grujdzak about it."

"We're old friends," I said.

"Friends, huh?"

"Well, Jo-Anne Stedman was a friend of mine," I said. "She considered herself responsible for the theft of certain important scientific papers and for another murder..."

"We know about that one too. Phyllis Kirk. Keep talking."

"It bothered her, so she went looking."

"And got killed for it? Chase, why can't you people realize we get paid to look and have been doing it for years and can do it much better than you? It would save an awful lot of trouble."

"I felt I ought to do something for Jo-Anne. Not hunt me a killer or anything like that," I lied. "Like you say, that's your department. But I thought I could get those papers back."

"That's interesting. How?"

"Through Guido. He had contacts you'd give your eyeteeth for. He called me to Brooklyn and you know the rest."

"Did he give you anything solid?"

I couldn't answer that until I found out how much the police knew. I said, "What about the murder car?"

"Stolen," the fat cop said at once. "No lead there. What did Guido have for you?"

"Well, Guido took me outside..."

"In front of The House That Jack Built?"

"That's right. I think he was going to tell me something, but he never got the chance."

"The car came around the corner of Avenue H and they killed Guido and hit you in the shoulder. That much, we know. That's all you know?"

"I took Guido's gun and ran after them."

"Oh. It was Guido's .45."

"Of course it was," I said. "What did you think?"

"And you don't know what he had in mind when he sent for you?"

They were crowding me. I could tell them what Guido had had in mind: two goons left over from the old days of Murder, Inc. Or I could tell them nothing. An image of Jo-Anne lying there, battered and dead, under the tarpaulin on Wompler's old boat, was conjured up inside my head. Another image, of Guido with a hand in front of his face, trying to stop the bullets, joined it. I shook my head and said, "I haven't the faintest idea."

"Chase, listen. Three floaters already. For your sake, I hope you told us all you know. No one who ever committed three murders will shy away from a fourth. You ought to realize that."

"I realize it. I hope what I told you has been of some help."

"Frankly, not much. We'll probably be back some time soon after we check things with Grujdzak and Manhattan West. Get well now, hear?"

"You give my regards to my good friend Pop Grujdzak."

One shrugged. One snickered. Fatso shook his head. Pop must have given them a lot of dirty words about me.

"Listen, guys," I said. "Maybe you could tell me this. After the Kirk kid was killed, I heard a cop say fingerprints were all over the place. I want to ask you—whose prints?"

"Jo-Anne Stedman's prints," the fat cop said.

"Nobody else's?"

"Yours, Chase. Hers and yours."

He turned and marched out of the room followed by the two tall guys.

I sat up against the pillow and thought hard.

All right, so none of Phyllis Kirk's prints had been found there—though she lived in the place.

That meant the apartment had been wiped of all prints before Jo-Anne and I had arrived. That was why the killer had hung around after the murder—to wipe. Probably he had been busy wiping away when he had heard Jo-Anne and me fumbling at the door. I pictured his movements in my mind. To make sure we wouldn't be able to see him, he had rushed to the fuse box in the kitchen, had loosened a fuse or two, but hadn't finished the job because we'd interrupted by entering. But in the darkness, he had managed to conk me.

Who?

* * * *

On Saturday, Ken and Julia came to visit me, bringing candy and flowers and wearing get-well-soon smiles.

"Damn them," Ken boomed. "Where did they hurt you? How does it feel, boy? There ought to be police on every corner in a neighborhood like that."

"Then you know what happened?"

"We read about it in the papers," Julia said. "Poor Jason."

"Everything's going to be all right now," Ken assured her. "We'll get Jason out of here and into a good hospital and…"

"The hell you will," I said. I was thinking about what the doctor had told me. The city gets rid of its patients in a hurry. "I'm comfortable right here."

"But in a charity ward!"

"It isn't charity," I told him, grinning. "When the city finds out who my brother is, they'll send a bill big enough to choke a horse."

Ken shrugged. "I'll pay anything to get you well."

"Hell, it's only a flesh wound. I just fell, that's all."

"You don't have to be heroic in front of me," Ken said. "I'll understand. Let your hair down, boy. Does a man good."

Talking with Ken was suddenly like wallowing neck deep in syrup. I listened while he oozed on about how a place was waiting for me with the construction company if I changed my mind and how he hadn't forgotten about the hundred thousand dollars, even if I had. Mention of the money made Julia's eyes go big and round, and she turned away quickly as if it wasn't right for her husband to keep talking about giving away that kind of money after it had been turned down, even if their relationship was miles away from what people had in mind when they spoke of happy marriages.

After fifteen minutes of it, I started hoping they would leave, but they stayed a full hour and then promised to return on Sunday.

But Stephanie was the first to arrive on Sunday afternoon. She smiled at me and plunked herself down on the foot of the bed and said, "They tell me you'll have to be in bed another few days."

"I'm leaving tomorrow."

"You listen to me, Jason. You stay here until you're well. There's nothing you have to do that can't wait, you hear me?"

"I'm deaf," I said. "But you know what I keep feeling like doing? Like kissing you, Steffy."

First she smiled, then she scowled, then she smiled again, showing her dimples. She had rosy cheeks and red lips and that beret perched atop her head. "That can be arranged," she said. She leaned forward and brushed her lips across my cheek, then stood up. "Now stay in bed till the doctor lets you up."

"Bribery, huh?"

It was the perfume. It was her eyes. It was her voice, the way she spoke. It was the way she stood and how she held her head on one side looking at you and wore the beret on the other side to balance things. It was everything.

Love that gal, I told myself. Aloud I said:

"Steffy, how do you feel about me?"

She knew what I meant. She smiled and squeezed my hand. "I'll have to sleep on it."

It cut me a little. "Do that."

"Get well, Jason!" She blew me a kiss from the doorway and then she was gone.

* * * *

My surprise visitor on Monday was Emma Grujdzak. "I see Steffy wasn't exaggerating," she said. "You look fit as a fiddle."

"That's what I keep telling the doc. Hey, does that mean Steffy's back home again?"

"It means nothing of the sort, young man, thanks to you."

"Pop won't forgive Steffy?"

"You know Pop. He builds things up inside his head. Pretty soon he'll get to thinking she wants to marry you or something."

I lay there and smiled. "I'm thinking, too."

"Jason Chase, I'll clobber you with this umbrella. Now, seriously, I came to see you about something Steffy found out." She'd stopped smiling. "It's something I think you ought to know. But don't tell Steffy I told you. She'd skin me alive."

"I'm listening."

"You want to know who's blackmailing your brother Ken?"

"You mean Wompler?"

"No, your brother Ken."

"Yeah, but…?"

"I told you. Kenneth Lamar Chase is blackmailing himself."

"Now wait a minute, Emma. Nobody blackmails himself. It doesn't figure. It doesn't make sense."

"I might have known that would be your reaction. There's lots more I could tell you, but if you…"

"Keep talking," I pleaded. "Can you prove it?"

"Not me. But I think Steffy can. She told me that Julia knew this Wilson Wompler person back in the old days and took up with him again later. Your brother Ken somehow learned that Wompler—well, you know—with Julia, I mean. Steffy's guess is that Wompler had no imagination and asked your brother what it was worth to Ken to keep it quiet and away from the newspaper people. Your brother must have got to thinking."

"Emma, it sounds silly."

"No. Things had gone sour between Julia and Ken. I'm no psychologist, or anything like that, but your brother Ken is a peculiar person. Julia confided in me once, right after you went to jail, and said Ken was really guilty and you were taking the rap for him."

"Julia never should have told you that."

"Well, is it true?" Emma demanded severely.

"Never mind. Just keep talking."

"All right. Assuming it true, it would take one queer duck of a man to send his own brother to jail and then go on talking all the time he was away about how you were always a wild kid and really meant well but he should have watched you more carefully. He owed it to the community, was what he said."

"So?"

"That's how he is. He'd die for his place in the community. It's the same way he treats Julia… He doesn't love her. Oh, maybe there was a time he thought he did, but now he's just afraid of what the neighbors would think, what all his snooty friends and people he knows would say behind his back if it was ever found out Julia had been unfaithful to him. He can't let it happen again, don't you see? So he made an arrangement with this Wompler person to blackmail him."

"Still too deep for me. I don't get it, Emma."

"You see, that's how he keeps Julia in line. He beats her with the blackmail. He makes believe he's suffering and paying this Wompler a fortune. He says if she doesn't behave, he'll stop paying, and the story will be out in all the papers. She won't do it again, not with Wompler, anyway."

"You say Steffy has proof?"

"Here's the most fantastic part of it. The first time, Wompler must have gone to your brother with nothing but his word. You can't very well blackmail a man without proof. So for a long time Ken made believe the pictures existed, only there weren't any pictures. He just told Julia there were. Then Steffy had to help her sister and wound up making everything that much simpler for Ken. Anyhow, Steffy went to work at Wompler's to see if she could get the pictures back. Just this Friday, she found them."

"I thought you said there weren't any pictures."

"She went snooping around in Wompler's office and found a file marked Kenneth Chase. There was a negative and a few prints and at first Steffy didn't get it. Maybe you know Wompler does some of his own modeling, to cut down on expenses. These were some shots Wompler had modeled with Steffy soon after she started working there. With Steffy!"

"Damn," I said. "You mean they weren't pictures of Julia at all?"

"That's right. Steffy recalls how she modeled those scenes with Wompler herself. Something for one of his girlie-girlie magazines about how to kiss in twenty-five different ways. But the pictures were never used. It was all part of Ken's game to blackmail himself. You know the resemblance between those two girls, their faces and how they're built and all. From a distance or a three-quarter side view with a lot of shadows, you could hardly tell the difference. Now Ken had pictures he could show Julia, probably just giving her an occasional peek at them."

"All right, so Wompler took phony pictures with Steffy. That still doesn't prove Ken arranged it himself."

"The heck it doesn't, young man. Excuse me. You see, Ken must have lent Wompler some of Julia's fanciest lingerie for the purpose. Staying at Ken's and Julia's place, Steffy saw the same frilly drawers and things—excuse me—that she wore in the pictures! It was enough to convince *her*—"

I rolled it around in my mind. I said, "At least she can call it quits at Wompler's now."

"Not that girl. Not on your life. Now she's determined to get the pictures. She was interrupted before she could take them on Friday."

"Why doesn't she just let Julia worry about her own problems?"

"Why did you go to prison for Ken?"

"That's different."

"You're a couple of young fools if you ask me, throwing your lives away like that. You, you're worse than Steffy."

It made sense, all of it. Almost too much sense. Steffy and Julia *did* look enough alike. With his mixed-up values, Ken *could* do something like that. Steffy had placed herself smack in the middle.

"What are you going to do about it, Jason Chase?"

I sat up. I started hollering for the nurse. "First I'm going to get out of here," I told Emma. "And thanks for letting me know."

Emma climbed into her fleece-collared storm coat and tested her umbrella tentatively at the door. She smiled at me again and then was gone. A few minutes later I was arguing with a couple of doctors. I was still a patient. My humerus and scapula still needed some mending. Did I lead an active life? I'd rip the bones apart again and all the city's work would be for naught. Let me worry about that, I said. They're my bones. Yes, I'd sign a release, any kind of release. The hospital wouldn't be responsible, nor the ward doctor, nor anyone. Where was my clothing?

The doctors and my nurse wandered off into the hallway and conferred in stage whispers. He's irresponsible. He's a glutton for punishment. We'll have to call his people and see if they can make arrangements to have him cared for at home. He'll be back. They always come back if they leave too soon. I should have taken up my Uncle Everett and gone into private practice with him. These charity cases. But doctor, don't you know who his brother is? The construction tycoon, Kenneth Lamar Chase. I might have known. Spoiled. You call his people, nurse.

An hour later, she deposited an offering of suit, topcoat, shirt, tie, underwear, socks and shoes on my bed in stony silence. The clothing was Ken's naturally, and as I dressed and tested the stiffness in my left arm, I began to wonder. The arm couldn't have punched its way through a wet Kleenex tissue.

I said goodbye to Plaster Cast on the other bed and marched out toward the elevator on wobbly legs, nodding to the patients who stood out in the hallway in their blue hospital robes, smoking and talking.

Downstairs, the waiting rooms were crowded with cold, soggy people. I crossed the floor to a window and watched the rain pelting down against it. I was on the point of hunkering down in my coat and trying my luck outside when someone tapped my shoulder.

I turned around and saw Steffy smiling at me.

"I've slept on it," she said.

Chapter Thirteen

She was wearing a beige raincoat and a colorful scarf covering her short brown hair. Her cheeks were rosy from contact with the cold outside. I stood there looking and waiting and not saying a word. I was suddenly all choked up inside. Me. The guy who was going to scare the pants off Wompler and get those pictures and who was going to do a slower, more thorough job than the police on Puggie and Five O'Clock.

Steffy placed her hands on my shoulders and held me off at arm's length. "For a guy who's been in bed a few days, you're looking great."

"I don't know how I feel yet. It's up to you."

"Silly. Kiss me and find out."

We tried it there in the waiting room, but there were too many people watching. We swung a quarter-turn in the revolving door and tried it again. This worked fine until someone wanted to go through so we found ourselves outside in the chill rain, with Steffy opening a big black man-style umbrella over our heads, where we tried it again.

"I'll have to admit I didn't really sleep on it, darling. I couldn't sleep. I was thinking and thinking about you all night."

"I love you, Steffy."

"That's what I've been trying to say, Jason. I'm in love with you. Oh, I love you so!"

And then we were exchanging words like darling and sweetheart and honey and all the others which seem so unreal and foolish until you want to use them, and then no other words seem so important or beautiful and you want to pound your chest because the girl you love loves you.

"Now you listen to me, honey," Steffy finally said, pouting. "I don't want you getting hurt, but I know you're out to get whoever stole those papers."

"Damned right I am," I mumbled against her hair.

"You mean, you used to be. Let's not have our first argument right now, so you just forget all about it and let the police…"

"Your old man? Are you crazy? Sweetheart, I'm sorry but you wouldn't want me like that. A coward."

"You wouldn't be a coward to let the police do police work."

"Forget it. I'll do what I have to."

"But—"

"Which reminds me. A kid like you shouldn't go around sticking her nose into other people's blackmail. I don't think you ought to go back to Wompler's. Model gloves or something."

"Gloves, the man says. With my equipment?"

"Well, that's not the point. Only don't go back there, that's all. Promise?"

"No!"

We stood glaring at each other, with the rain pummeling the big umbrella over our heads. Steffy smiled first. Then we were laughing and the umbrella was bobbing up and down.

"Look," I began again. "This is different. You're a girl."

"I'm so close to getting those pictures now, I wouldn't promise to stop even if you promised me that you'd stop."

"I'm not doing this for Ken," I pointed out. "I'm doing it for myself and for a little guy named Guido who never had a chance and for a girl named Jo-Anne who was the most wonderful kid in the world. Except you. But I don't owe Ken a thing. Do you realize I spent two years in jail for that guy while he went scot free?"

"Hah!"

"He was desperate. He said he had to keep the business going. He was a cripple; I had crippled him. He couldn't take it in jail, he said. I was young. A hundred thousand bucks he'd give me. I owed him this, he said. He pleaded. I was nuts."

"But that's different. That was criminal."

"No more criminal than you stealing photos—"

"Jason Chase, Emma's been here to see you. Wait till I get hold of her, just wait!"

"You're making the same mistake I made a couple of years ago. Getting yourself in trouble for a brother. I mean, a sister—"

"Call it what you want, but I've got to be able to live with myself." She headed down the steps. "I'm not sore or anything, Jason.

It's just got to be this way. We each have a job we have to get done. Listen, I drove down in Ken's car. Can I drop you somewhere in Manhattan?"

I gave her Tad Barrett's address as we walked toward Ken's big Lincoln. I offered to drive but Steffy said, "The power steering's like dialing a telephone." She gunned the motor and we were off. She sat peering through the big one-piece windshield and swishing wipers. She was enjoying herself like a little girl, like a high-school kid with his first jalopy. Hell, she was only twenty. All the way down Bedford Avenue to the Williamsburg Bridge I wished I could knock some sense into her. She was probably wishing she could do the same to me.

* * * *

Tad Barrett seemed surprised to see me.

"Jason Chase! I read what happened to you. I thought you'd be in the hospital a while yet." He palmed the dottle from his pipe and shook hands with me. "Sit down. I've got a little news for you, but you won't like it."

"I've plenty to tell you," I said, "but let's hear your's first."

"That poor kid Stedman must have talked before they killed her."

"Yeah? What makes you think so?"

"Three new clients visited me today, all about the same thing. The Kincaid papers. They'd received threats of blackmail about some of their answers to the professor's questions. If you know anything about those questions, you know why they couldn't go to the police."

I nodded and waited.

"I wanted to be sure, so I called a couple of friends of mine in the shamus racket. The same thing. It's all over town and it means a lot of trouble for a lot of people."

Barrett swiveled around in his chair and pulled a file drawer open. He withdrew a folder with the one word *Kincaid* on the file tab and shoved it across the desk at mo. He'd made copies of three blackmail letters and I lit a cigarette and studied them.

The first one went:

Mr. Drew Greer,
Greer Export Company

New York, New York

I have in my possession your answers to the Kincaid questionnaire for the forthcoming book, *Twentieth Century Morality*.

No doubt your wife would be interested in learning what really happened in Montevideo in January of last year.

Also, the Federal Government probably would like to learn how an importer manages to bring South African diamonds to the United States tariff-free, via South America.

I am not a hasty man. No one has this information but myself, and the Kincaid people, of course. Is it worth $25,000 to you? I will contact you again.

There was no signature.

Barrett shook his head grimly. "Greer's big," he said. "His import-export business is worth millions and from what he tells me his record is spotlessly clean. Or was spotlessly clean."

"Why do people like that take a chance answering the Kincaid questionnaire?"

"Why?" Barrett shrugged. "Why does a man do anything? Maybe it's like a big financier who makes a fortune legally but amorally, then decides to give a few million bucks anonymously to charity. Maybe Greer and the others figured this would be a worthy cause, exposing certain trends without getting themselves personally involved. Of course, the publicity surrounding the Kinsey books helped. Everyone knew the research work was coded. Everyone was sure it was safe. No one dreamed he was answering deadly questions. How many times have you heard people say they wished Kinsey—or now, Kincaid—would interview *them*!"

I looked at the other letters. They were essentially the same, with only the names and incidents changed. I recognized the name of a young legislator on the way up, a man his party was grooming for the governor's mansion or, some said, Capitol Hill. Barrett told me the third man owned a seat on the stock exchange.

"These men could scrape together twenty-five thousand each without too much trouble," Barrett explained. "But they're afraid the blackmailer won't stop at that figure. My guess is he won't, either."

I was thinking of Jo-Anne again, all alone and crying for help that night on South Street. They'd hurt her and made her talk, then killed her. Puggie and Five O'Clock? Guido thought so—and got himself killed for thinking it. It wasn't just Puggie and Five O'Clock, though. They were fungus; garden-variety thugs. There had to be someone behind them. Wompler? Could be; but if Emma was right, Wompler didn't even have the brains to blackmail Ken successfully, and had to settle for helping Ken blackmail himself.

"Barrett," I said, "when I first mentioned Wompler, you acted like you never heard of the guy—"

"Should I have?"

"My brother hired you to locate some shakedown pictures, didn't he? You mean to say he never told you about Wompler?"

Barrett laughed. "Look, let's get this straight. You're Ken's brother, so I guess I can tell you. He didn't hire me to look for pictures. He's paying me to *pretend* to look for them. He let it be known to his wife—and some others, I guess—that he's put this agency on the trail. If anyone queries me about it, I'm supposed to say yes, I'm on the case, and making progress."

"And you take work like that?"

He shrugged. "It's a living."

"Barrett," I said, "there's something else. That man of yours who visited Wompler's apartment. Did he ever report anything about picking up Jo-Anne there?"

"You asked me that night. He's a good man. Working for me twelve years. He says he never even saw Jo-Anne, and I believe him."

All right, I thought, so Wompler was a liar. But Audrey—did she love Wompler so hard that she would lie too? Was she maybe playing little games of her own—games with the Kincaid papers?

"What do you have to tell me?" Barrett was saying.

"Plenty. First, my brother's sister-in-law is on her way to Wompler's about the blackmail pictures Ken hired you not to find. Second, Guido had something, all right. He smelled out two hoods, Puggie LaBetta and Five O'Clock McGuire. They killed him for it." I gave Barrett the details of what happened that night. "So far," I went on, "Wompler's my only other lead. He was supposed to be blackmailing my brother…"

"Was?"

"It's a long story. Anyhow, he knew Phyllis Kirk. He knew about the Kincaid papers, even knew she had them. I've got to follow it up, and I intend to. I came here because I was wondering if you knew anything about LaBetta and McGuire."

"We keep a little rogues' gallery of our own on file so I can use my police contacts for more important things. Let's take a look."

Barrett led the way into another room, its walls lined from floor to ceiling with file drawers. "No LaBetta," he said a few minutes later, handing me an old newspaper clipping which included the police lineup picture of a man. "Here's your Five O'Clock McGuire, though."

The clipping was about a young gunsel the D.A.'s office was looking for in connection with extortion. The thug's name was James (Five O'Clock) McGuire and there was a picture to prove it. Five O'Clock had a long narrow face; his jaw was enormous, with a scar starting at the left corner of his bloodless lips and getting lost in the shadow under the right side of his angrily jutting chin.

"Think you could recognize him?" Barrett asked. "That was twelve years ago."

"Unless they did plastic surgery on that scar since then, I'll know him. Guy about your age, thirty-five, thirty-six? Yeah, when I see him I'll know it."

I thanked Barrett and went outside to wait for the elevator.

I felt the need of something warm to drink because my muscles were suddenly tired and aching a little and I could feel a chill coming on. First I thought it was only because I'd been in bed a few days, then I suspected I was coming down with a cold. Well, you could catch worse things in the hospital.

I got my first *gesundheit* from the elevator operator in Wompler's office building.

Chapter Fourteen

Wompler wasn't in, but I found Audrey posing for the photographer as a white amazon reared by the matriarchal Tchambuli tribe of green-jungled New Guinea, meeting an explorer from Boston for the first time. The jungle set, I decided, might look convincing enough in black and white, but the explorer was something straight out of Abercrombie & Fitch, and Audrey had borrowed her leopard-skin leotards and long blonde hair from the pages of Congo Comics. She held a prop knife in her hand and the explorer was teaching her one of the more subtle arts of Boston society, known as smooching.

"So now they've got leopards in New Guinea," I said, reading the location data off the photographer's info sheet.

"If it isn't Mr. Chase," Audrey said tartly. "Are you married?"

"No, but..."

"I was thinking if you were you probably wouldn't peek so much."

"I don't see Wompler around," I said.

"He just went out."

"Well, I also wanted to see you."

"You're seeing."

"Alone."

"Do I have to?"

"You don't have to do anything. I have something to tell you, that's all."

"About what?"

"Your boyfriend, Wompler."

Audrey's gaze was level and steady. "Come on," she finally said. "We can use his office."

I followed the leopard-dotted leotards into Wompler's office and watched Audrey sit down, crossing her long, sturdy legs. There was a lot of leg visible, because if you take a T-shirt and sew the middle of the hem together for a crotch, that's a pair of leotards.

"I try to mind my own business," Audrey told me, "but you keep asking Willie things about blackmail. A girl gets curious."

"That's what I wanted to talk about."

"You're not going to start swinging?"

"Listen, Audrey. This was strictly between Wompler and me, but you poked your two cents in…"

"You said you wanted to tell me something."

"I'm just explaining why you got shoved, that's all. You're damned right I want to tell you something. You've got a crush on Wompler, haven't you?"

"I don't see where that's any of your business. Why don't you wait here, if you want to see Willie? Or come back later?" Audrey uncrossed her thighs and stood up. It was going to be now, right now, or our interview would end almost before it got under way.

"Willie's been making time with another woman," I said.

Audrey sat down hard and didn't bother to cross her legs. She slouched over, let her arms dangle between her thighs, laced her fingers there and stared at them. "You'd better tell me the rest of it," she said sullenly.

"That's where the blackmail comes in. Willie made it with a gal named Julia Chase."

"Your sister?"

"My sister-in-law."

"Listen here, mister. If you're making this up, you're going to wish you never came here."

I gave her one version of it.

"Listen. Willie was blackmailing my brother, Julia's husband. He's a pretty big wheel and he couldn't afford the kind of bad publicity Willie could give him. The shakedown was possible because Julia—"

"You don't have to say any more." The long fingers untwined, formed fists, smashed down on the flesh of the thighs. "Just get out of here."

"There's more I want to tell you."

"Get out! Please get out."

"Uh-uh. You know Steffy Grujdzak?"

Audrey looked like a big, graceful jungle animal trapped in her first cage. Maybe she did belong in New Guinea and leotards at that. "She's a good kid. Don't tell me he also slept with her!"

"Hell, no. Steffy is Julia Chase's sister." I told Audrey how Steffy had come to work at Wompler's with the idea of somehow putting a stop to the blackmail, then wound up contributing to it by posing for pictures which could be used as proof of her sister's adultery.

"That's a coincidence," Audrey said.

"What is?"

"Steffy was in this office with Willie right before you came in. Not fifteen minutes ago. I was outside on Set Five, so I could hear. They talked for a while, then Willie got a phone call. He acted like he wasn't happy over the message, but he hung up and made a phone call of his own. Then he left—with Steffy."

"What were they talking about?"

"I couldn't hear the words. Only that Willie sounded upset."

"Where did they go?"

"Search me, Mr. Chase."

I sneezed. Audrey God-blessed me. I honked my nose. The cold was in full flower.

In the back of my mind, something was nibbling, trying to clamp its teeth and catch hold. Something that would answer a lot of questions, something I should have known but didn't. It was like trying to remember the name of someone you'd met casually years ago. I lit a cigarette and tried to think. The smoke scraped against my throat harshly and made me sneeze again. My head was big as a balloon but heavy as lead. The thing was on the tip of my mental tongue but wouldn't allow itself to be spat out.

"Try to remember," I pleaded with Audrey. "Didn't you hear anything of his phone conversation?"

"Just the tone of his voice."

"Damn! Did he say he was coming back later?"

"He's got to come back. He wants to do some paste-ups for the next issue of *Hush*."

"When?"

"Tonight, probably. He often works at night. Are you going to wait for him?"

I looked at my watch. Quarter to six. Through the window I could see it was dark outside already. The rain had finally lost its fight with the temperature and turned to snow. Elsewhere in the loft of an office I could hear Wompler's hired hands bustling about and getting ready to leave. "Let me make a couple of phone calls," I said. "Then we'll see."

Audrey nodded and stuck around to listen while I dialed Ken's apartment and spoke to Julia. "This is Jason," I said. "I was wondering if Steffy's home."

"No. I thought she was with you, Jason."

"She was earlier. You don't know where she is?"

"Probably delayed by the snow. She drives Ken's Lincoln like a motor bike, though. I hope she's careful. Why don't you come on over and wait here for her, Jason?"

I said no, and jabbed at the phone cradle with my fingers until I got another dial tone. Then I dialed again and heard Emma Grujdzak say, "Hello?" I was glad it wasn't Pop. Steffy wasn't there, either.

"Listen," I said, debating with myself and coming up with an answer I didn't like. "As soon as Pop gets home, have him call this number." I gave her Wompler's Plaza number. "Tell him it's about these murders and the Kincaid papers. Tell him he'd damned well better call as soon as he comes in the door."

"Steffy is in trouble, isn't she?"

"Don't worry, Emma. Don't you worry. I won't let anything happen to Steffy. Promise." Yeah, promise. Right now, all I could do was sit on my duff and wait for something to happen.

"Are you sticking around?" Audrey asked me when I hung up.

"Yeah, I'll wait."

"Good. If you were lying before, me and Willie are going to break your neck."

"And if I was telling the truth?"

"Then you and me are going to break Willie's neck."

"It's all yours," I said. "I only want information."

Audrey called downstairs for some supper, and when I wanted to pay for it she said it could go on expenses. Audrey ate daintily, but still managed to put down four sandwiches while I was picking away at two liverwursts on rye which tasted like exactly nothing— me and my stuffed nose!

It was a long wait, but finally Wompler walked in. At seven fifty-five.

I jumped up.

Audrey jumped up.

"Where the hell did you take Steffy?" I shouted at the top of my voice.

"What kind of business is this, you playing around with Julia Chase?" Audrey screamed.

We hollered simultaneously, and Wompler didn't get it. He knew something was wrong, though. He looked at me and looked at Audrey and turned around, heading for the door. Audrey pounced across the room and blocked the door with a little leopard skin and a lot of Audrey skin.

"He says you've been making time," she told her Willie.

He looked small next to her, almost as small as Guido.

"To hell with that," I said. "Where's Steffy? Where'd you take her?"

"You," Wompler said, pointing a finger at me, "are getting to be a nuisance. Audrey, if you throw that bum out of here, I can explain everything."

I grabbed the damp lapels of Wompler's coat and shook him. For a time we listened to the change rattling in his pockets, then I let go and said, "Start talking."

He might have, but then Audrey followed my example and shook him.

"You got a phone call," I said, "then you made one. After that, you went out with Steffy. Where is she?"

"Deny it about Julia Chase, you no-good little rat!" Audrey cried, still shaking him.

I locked the door and then gently but firmly got hold of Audrey's wrists and pulled her away.

"Sit down and listen," I said. I wasn't fooling now. There was no time. I sneezed and shoved Audrey in the general direction of a chair. I rapped my knuckles against Wompler's mouth. His head bobbed like a punching bag and he began to whimper. I was sure Audrey could do the job just as well but it might take her longer. I slammed Wompler against the locked door and waited until he bounced back and rapped his mouth again. A thin trickle of blood had emerged from the corner of his lips, running down over his chin. His eyes begged me to stop but his teeth were clamped together defiantly, so I kept at it.

After a while, he slumped forward in my arms. He didn't seem to weigh more than his suit and coat and maybe a good pair of brogans. Suddenly his head came up and butted my chin, making me bite my tongue. I yowled and yowled again when he kicked my shin and whirled around, clawing at the door. Before he could open it I got him by the scruff of the neck and pounded his face against the paneled door with the words Wilson Wompler, Publisher, stenciled on the reverse side.

I wasn't feeling proud of myself and began wondering how long Wompler would remain silent. His head made a dull noise against the wood and the door shook in its frame. I spun him around and let go. He slumped to the floor in a sitting position and Audrey got a paper cupful of ice water from the cooler and splashed it in his face.

"Can you hear me?" I said. "Start by giving me those pictures."

"What pictures?"

"You know goddamned well what pictures."

"I'm going to break your neck if you were lying, mister," Audrey promised me.

Wompler supplied her answer by staggering to his desk and retrieving a folder from the bottom drawer. He mopped the blood from his lips with a monogrammed handkerchief and handed me the folder. "I'm through," he said. "You Chase boys are a couple of nuts. First he wants me to blackmail him, then you say he doesn't want. Then he says it's all a mistake, I should go on blackmailing him. Then you come here to kill me if I don't give you the pictures. I'm all through with you crazy people. Oh, God, Audrey! Please listen to me! I can explain."

He was trying to explain while I took a quick look at the pictures. There were several glossy four-by-five prints of a shot which bordered on the pornographic but didn't quite make it. It was Steffy all right, not Julia—but you had to study the picture a while to tell. The lighting was dim and you could see Wompler clearly in his silk pajamas but Steffy in Julia's lingerie was in shadow. She'd posed in all innocence, I was sure. Making her fifteen bucks an hour for a series on how to kiss your lover or some such thing which was never intended for use in Wompler's magazines. I stuffed the prints and negative in the inside pocket of my jacket, figuring I'd burn them in front of Julia and then let her decide what to do next.

A frightened Wompler stood behind the desk, ready to dart either way. Audrey was in front of the desk, leaning over and shaking her fist at him. "You're a one-woman man, huh? I'm the only girl in your life, huh? There used to be a lot of fish in the sea but you threw away your rod and reel when you found me, huh? And I swallowed all of it, hook, line and sinker. I'm going to break your two-timing little neck, you lousy rat!"

Then the phone rang.

Wompler regarded it as a *deus ex machina*, but backed away when Audrey reached for it and shouted, "Hello?" She nodded, "Yes, he's here. It's for you, Mr. Chase."

I reached her in two quick strides and brought the phone to my ear. "Pop?" I said.

"This is Grujdzak. What do you want, Chase?" His voice was colder than the snow falling outside. "Isn't that Wilson Wompler's number you had me call?"

"I'm here with Wompler," I said. "I haven't time to talk much, so you better just listen."

"Don't tell me what to do."

"Just shut your yap and listen, dammit, unless you don't care what happens to your daughter Steffy."

"Steffy?"

"I'm at Wompler's, getting some information out of him. He left Steffy some place, I don't know where. She may be in trouble."

"I don't see what Steffy has to do with..."

"Julia was being blackmailed by Wompler." That was part of the truth. The rest would come out in the wash. I didn't have time to explain. "Steffy tried to stop him and got herself in hot water."

"Where is she? Chase, if any harm comes...

"That's what I'm trying to prevent. You get on over here soon as you can. I probably won't be around, but Wompler will be in good hands and you'll be told where to go." He was rasping and spluttering when I hung up.

"All right," I said to Wompler, "no more fooling around. Where'd you take her?"

"Oh, God, they'll kill me."

"Not who. Just where."

Audrey had him cornered behind the desk, which she had shoved toward one wall as a barricade. His only way out of the corner led right into Audrey's arms.

"I'll tell you! I'll tell you if you get this crazy woman out of here."

"Talk."

"It's in Brooklyn, that's all I know. I delivered Miss Grujdzak to a man named McGuire. They made me do it, Chase. I knew too much, they said. I saw what they could do."

I shouldered Audrey aside. At first she looked as if she wanted to contest the right to reach Wompler first but she saw what was in my eyes and changed her mind. I got to Wompler and my right fist didn't travel ten inches but it had everything I felt about Jo-Anne and Guido and Steffy behind it. Wompler bounced off the window frame and fell forward on his face, not moving.

"Stay with him," I told Audrey. "There's a cop, Grujdzak, Steffy's father, who should be here soon. You tell him I went after a guy named Five O'Clock McGuire, in Brooklyn. And don't let Willie out of here. The cops will want to hold him as an accomplice in the Kincaid business."

"He's no good, huh?"

"He's a stinking son who…"

"I get the idea. The lousy rat!"

I opened the door and waved bye-bye to the lady who crouched near Wompler's still form, ready to put him back to sleep as soon as his eyelids fluttered.

I called over my shoulder, "Hey, do you have a car I could use? Steffy's up to her neck in trouble."

Audrey got up and padded barefoot to her street clothes hanging on a rack in Wompler's office. She tossed me a chain of keys and said, "It's a blue Plymouth coupe parked down near the corner." She went back into her crouch.

As soon as I hit the street I began to sneeze again. The cold air cleared my stuffed head some, but my nose started running. I wished I could hole up somewhere with hot lemonade and brandy and a lot of blankets. I found Audrey's Plymouth, climbed inside and listened to the motor growl. I shifted into first and pulled away from the curb and got the lights and wipers working. It was now eight-twenty. The chills hit me and I turned on the heater. It was snowing hard. I headed south through the slippery streets, point-ing the Plymouth toward the Williamsburg Bridge and The House That Jack Built.

Of course, they might have taken her to Livonia Street. But I played my hunch.

Chapter Fifteen

The snow had driven people to cover and there was something unreal about the cars parked on Avenue H, white with their mantles of snow. I listened and heard nothing but the crunching sound of the Plymouth's tires as I coasted to the curb and parked. I got out and hurried through the snow toward Nostrand Avenue.

One whiff of stale beer and smoke assailed my nostrils before the warm air inside the place clogged my head again. There was a crowd at the bar, watching two bald fat men wrestle on the television screen. The booths were filled with younger people of both sexes who seemed to have only recently graduated from the luncheonette down the street.

I squeezed between a couple of big guys at the bar who were grunting and groaning in sympathy with the actors cavorting on the TV screen.

"Hey," I said.

"A minute, Mac." The barman was busy wiping heads from three glasses of tap beer.

"This is important."

He slid the glasses along the bar and came over, wiping his hands on a dirty towel. "What'll it be?"

"McGuire," I said. "Where is he?"

"I don't know no McGuire," he answered. "You want a drink or don't you?"

I grinned at him. "Come off it, stupid. I'm from Livonia Street. Five O'Clock wants to see me."

He appraised me while I worked my features into a scowl and said, "I don't have all night."

"Awright. Awright, take it easy. You guys don't hang around Livonia Street no more, you're going to see a lot of me. Might as well be friends, huh?"

Whatever Guido had predicted would go wrong on Livonia Street must have gone wrong in a hurry.

"McGuire," I said.

He jerked a thumb toward the rear of the place. "Upstairs. Tell Auntie it's awright. Louis says you're from Livonia Street to see Five O'Clock."

"I'll tell her, Louis."

I found the stairs behind the U-shaped bar. Auntie was sitting at a desk atop the stairs like the floor nurse at a hospital. I took one look at her and knew exactly what kind of a house Jack had built, and right here behind the city's college, too.

"What are you looking for, mister?" Auntie's voice was husky and completely indifferent.

"Well, it's not the john," I said nasally, and offered her what I hoped was a bona fide Livonia Street grin. Then I changed my mind in a hurry. Five O'Clock might be anywhere, lurking in the shadows in back of Auntie or behind one of the closed doors near by. He might hear me and he most definitely would be carrying a gun. I'd better do some looking around before I said I was from Livonia Street again.

"You know," I tried, "you know what." I chuckled and sniffed.

"Is that a bad cold you got?" Auntie was built like Tony Galento with an inflated bosom stuffed into a dress with life-size black-eyed susans printed all over it. A pencil protruded from her bunned hair and now she'd taken it out to run the point over a sheet of paper attached to a clipboard on her desk.

"Only a little allergy," I assured her.

"We don't like our girls catching cold, that's all. It's bad for business."

"Naw," I bleated. "Don't you worry."

Auntie consulted her clipboard once more. "Room four," she said, and took a metal strong-box from a drawer of her desk, opening it and revealing neat stacks of ten-dollar bills. I added one to the kitty, which just about broke me.

"Room four," Auntie repeated, and made a check on her clipboard.

My damp shoes creaked as I walked down the dimly lit hall. I found room four and stood outside for a few seconds, wondering what to do next. Obviously, I couldn't spend too much time with its occupant. I had to make her think I was something besides a paying customer. I didn't know what, though. Auntie's eyes were probably studying my back as I stood there. I didn't know if many of Auntie's customers got stage fright or not. I was a stranger here myself. I knocked on the door.

"It isn't locked." The voice was muffled and childish.

I opened the door and closed it swiftly behind me. She was just a kid. She looked tough and sulky but had solemn eyes. She wore a quilted kimona. She was barefoot with painted toenails and wore her dark hair in an upsweep. She sat there on a slip-covered wing chair across from the bed and couldn't have been older than Steffy. She was smoking a cork-tipped cigarette and had left deep red lipstick stains on it. A small phonograph on the night table was playing a scratchy rendition of *I'm In The Mood For Love*.

"Hello," she said. "I'm Doris."

"I'm Jason," I told her. By gosh, I was embarrassed.

"You can sit over here by me if you want, for a while." She patted the seat of the wing chair. She was letting me know they didn't believe in assembly-line speed at The House That Jack Built. A classy joint.

I walked to the chair and sat down. There was barely enough room for both of us and Doris swung one of her thighs over the arm of the chair. Her skin was very pale.

"Uh, listen, Doris. You've got this wrong. I…"

"You don't have to be shy, Jason." She didn't sound like she looked, which was tough. She swung her other leg over the arm of the chair, leaned back, and was resting against my lap and looking up at me.

"No, I mean I'm a reporter. A reporter from, uh, *Hush*. The magazine that prints all the facts."

"*Hush*! Say, I've heard of that."

"I'd like to interview you."

I stood up. It caught Doris by surprise and I leaned over awkwardly to catch her as she started to fall, but she yelped and tried to right herself by grabbing my arms. We both wound up on the floor. Doris' kimona had come open, revealing black bra and panties.

"I only want some facts," I said quickly as Doris got to her feet.

"Such as?"

"How many girls work here?"

"Well, there's Toni, Marie, Angy, Linda, Irene, Rhoda, Bertie and me. That's eight."

I couldn't get around to Five O'Clock at once. "How long does the average girl stay?"

"Which one of us is the average girl you mean?"

"How long have you been here?"

"Five months."

"Going to, uh, make it a career?" I was doing great.

"Say, are you crazy or something? You think I'm a creep?"

"Sorry. About how many customers, uh..."

"If you're a reporter, why aren't you taking notes like I seen them do on TV?"

"I have a good memory," I assured Doris.

"Maybe I ought to ask Auntie if it's all right."

"I already did. Do you ever have to perform any extracurricular activities?" I asked.

"Extra what?"

"Aside from your work. Like making bar guests comfortable or something like that."

"You know, it's a funny thing, you asking that." Doris now was lounging on the bed with her hands behind her head, making herself comfortable. She crossed her knees in air, one foot supporting her legs on the mattress, the other swinging gently back and forth. "I mean, a funny thing you asking it right now. I don't like them at all."

"You don't like who?"

"Those new guys. Louis says they work here and even Mr. Jack says so, but I haven't seen them do nothing. They just hang around and get smart and make all kinds of snotty remarks. Gimme a puff, willya, Jason?"

I crossed to the bed and held my cigarette to her lips. She steadied my wrist with her hands and took a long drag, then blew the smoke at me. I sneezed. "Say, you're a cold fish, Jason. You know it?"

"Strictly business," I said. "I'm interviewing you. About these new guys..."

"Yeah. They brung a new girl in with them, y'know. So maybe before I should have said nine."

"A girl? When?"

"Just today. A couple of hours ago. It was a little early for business so I was out in the hall talking to Auntie and Bertie when they come up with this new girl. Say, what do you keeping looking at the door for?"

"Who was she with?" I asked. "A guy about thirty-five, with a big scar on his chin? Always looks like he needs a shave?"

"Five O'Clock, the others call him. You know, it's a funny thing. First I thought they were talking about the time or something, only it's his name. Five O'Clock. You ever hear anything so nutty?"

"Where are Five O'Clock and the new girl now?"

"Say, is this part of the interview?"

"We will send a photographer around later," I said, sitting on the edge of the bed and patting Doris' shoulder. It was a mistake. She misunderstood the gesture and bounced into a sitting position, in the same motion reaching behind her with her hands and unhooking the bra.

"Go on with the interview, please," she said, and giggled.

I got up and walked to the wing chair and sat down. Doris was sitting cross-legged on the bed. "Don't you like me?" she pouted.

I said, "You are luscious. It will be written that way, luscious."

"Well?"

I sneezed. "I have a very bad cold, Doris."

"Say, then Auntie never should have let you come in here. She don't like colds."

I winked at Doris. "I told Auntie it was an allergy, so I could see you."

"Say, that's cute. An allergy!"

"About Five O'Clock and the new girl. Where are they?"

Doris waved her arms. "Somewhere up here, I don't know. Not in any of the numbered rooms, though. There's one each for Bertie, Angy, Marie…"

"I know." I got the door opened and peered outside. Auntie looked up from her desk and I ducked back into the room. Doris padded up behind me and whispered, "Close the door. Auntie says never keep the door open."

"I'll have to go now."

"We haven't finished the interview," Doris giggled again. "We haven't even started."

I looked outside again. Auntie was reading a magazine. I took two steps into the hall, but Doris followed, tugging at my arm.

"Hey!" she said. "Come on back."

Auntie looked up, then climbed to her feet and came streaking toward us as if she'd been shot from a gun. This despite her bulk, which was considerable.

"Get back inside!" she raged at us. "You know the rules."

She meant Doris. I didn't know the rules from a hole in the wall, but I was learning.

"Jason here is going to get all our pictures in the magazine. Aren't you, Jason?"

"Well, now…"

"What are you talking about?" Auntie demanded, looking at me suspiciously.

"He's a reporter from that magazine, *Hush*"

"He's giving you a line, you mean. Mister, who sent you here?"

"Louis said I could…"

"I mean, before Louis."

"Well, Five O'Clock suggested…"

"Five O'Clock?" Auntie gave me a grudging smile. "Why didn't you say so? I wish you boys would stop pulling my girls' legs, though. Oh, Mr. McGuire! Mr. McGuire!" Suddenly she was shouting. I wanted to hide. I grabbed Auntie's arm and raised a finger to my lips for silence. I sneezed.

A door opened, throwing a shaft of light into the hall. He came out, staring, and he was big; two or three inches taller than my own six feet. He was wide across the shoulders or he had a good tailor. His face was long and narrow and his enormous jaw was shaded a greasy blue from his heavy whiskers. A long scar, looking very white, ran across his jaw.

Five O'Clock McGuire, all right He was still staring, his eyes trying to grow accustomed to the dim light. I figured I had about ten seconds before we'd be evenly matched. I led my right fist down the hall at a trot and swung it around in front of me. It made a dull sound against Five O'clock's huge jaw and went numb to the elbow.

He roared and thudded back against the door jamb without going down, and I knew I was in for a fight. Auntie yelled, "I'll call the police!"

"You do and you'll wish you worked in the five-and-ten," Five O'Clock told her, then came for me.

I caught his left fist on my palm and brought up my shoulder to absorb the right cross which was blossoming toward me. I'd forgotten my wound and grunted as a sharp needle of pain stabbed through the left side of my body. Five O'Clock pressed forward, shuffling at me flatfooted. His eyes were fighter's eyes which could feint you out of position without a muscle moving.

I parried his left again, but with a shrewd animal instinct he made for the injured shoulder. I had to protect it and wound up on the receiving end of a right cross with plenty of leverage behind it. The hall tilted crazily, fat Auntie in her black-eyed susan dress, Doris with her open mouth and breasts heaving, and all. My back jarred the floor as I went down and I had time to think Louis must be worrying that one of the beds had collapsed. Then Five O'clock's shoe swam at me out of the dimness and the heel suspended there, ready to strike. I caught it flush in the mouth and spat blood, expecting teeth to follow.

I squirmed away and tried to get enough distance to climb to my feet, but the heel stamped down on my shoulder on the second try. The injured shoulder. I lay there throbbing with pain and cursing Five O'Clock, lifting my hands to ward off the next downthrust of his shoe. He came plowing at me sideways instead, kicking me in the ribs. I rolled over on my stomach and over again, clutching at Five O'clock's shoe and twisting it. He lost his balance and bellowed something Doris was never meant to hear, no matter what business she was in.

I pawed the waxed floorboards and struggled to my feet first, but Five O'Clock was not far behind. We stood there pummeling each other's guts and you could hear it, thud, thud, thud, and our harsh breathing, and nothing else. Then the bastard butted me with his head so hard I nearly bit the tip of my tongue clean off. Someone yowled. Me.

Five O'clock's knee came up between my legs and I thought, as I collapsed toward the floor, he had no respect for the Marquis of Queensbury. He took a deep breath and came hurtling down after me but I'd learned a couple of tricks myself in prison. I did a kick-up, the soles of my shoes catching him right under the rib cage, lifting him up and tossing him away.

He crashed into the wall and I was after him, getting in a couple of good pokes at his immense jaw before he slid down the wall to the floor. Afterwards my shoulder would ache like it wanted to fall off, but not now. Now I was thinking of Guido and Jo-Anne and Steffy. Also of myself.

I kicked Five O'Clock in the kidneys and listened to him scream. I kicked him in the chin, in the great jutting chin, and watched his head slam against the wall. I sank the toe of my shoe into his gut, exposed now, the muscles not tensed. His head lolled to the side and I kicked it, laying open the skin and flesh along one cheekbone and watching the blood splash down on his white shirt.

"Where's the girl?" I said.

Five O'Clock couldn't talk just yet. His mouth opened and closed but he only succeeded in drooling.

Doris crouched there, her skin glistening with sweat, trickles of it running down her chest and between her breasts. She looked like she both hated the fight and loved it. Auntie was gawking at me with new respect. Then footsteps came pounding up the stairs. Louis coming to investigate the ruckus, I thought, or Mr. Jack.

It wasn't Louis and I was willing to bet it wasn't Jack.

He was big and round and had a huge pig nose tip-tilted and spread over his face. His skin was swarthy and I figured he had a name: Puggie LaBetta. I whirled to face him but Five O'Clock had enough strength left to stick out his leg and trip me. I plummeted head first toward Puggie, off balance. He obliged by straightening me with a couple of left hooks and sitting me down alongside Five O'Clock with a right cross. Puggie used his dukes like he'd once fought professionally.

More feet pounded on the stairs. I sat numb, shaking my head, next to the bleeding Five O'Clock. Louis called, "Everything awright up there?"

"Hunky dory," Puggie told him. Louis retreated downstairs. I started scrambling to my feet, but Puggie kicked me in the chest.

Then he reached into his pocket, crouched alongside me and laid a sap across my forehead. I hardly felt it but I knew I was going to pass out. Doris opened her mouth to scream but I closed my eyes and shut my ears and chased the sound away.

CHAPTER SIXTEEN

It was a room, a lot like Doris' place of business, with a double bed, a wing chair, a bureau, an alcove leading off in the direction of the bathroom. All this I saw when I opened my eyes.

Then I saw Steffy.

"Don't talk," she said. "Don't try to get up. What did they do to you? I was so afraid you would…"

"Not this boy," I said. I sneezed. I'd been deposited on the floor and now I sat up.

"I think I stopped the bleeding," Steffy said. "They threw you in here about an hour ago, without saying a word. Jason, what do they want with us?"

"Tell me what happened after you went to see Wompler, then maybe we'll figure it out."

I touched the sore spots on my head gingerly and felt the caked blood there. I listened as Steffy spoke.

"First of all, stop looking at the door. It's locked from the outside."

I stopped looking at the door. I looked at Steffy instead and wound up kissing her. She was kneeling beside me and I pulled her down gently and could feel her trembling.

"I was so afraid, Jason."

"I love you, kid."

"I love you too."

She sighed. I sighed. I pushed her away and said, "So?"

"Well, I told Mr. Wompler I knew about the pictures. About how he had plotted with Ken to use a picture of me and make believe it was Julia so he could 'blackmail' your brother."

She stopped to kiss me.

"You'll catch cold," I warned.

"Mr. Wompler said the whole idea was your brother's. Then someone called him on the phone, and he called someone else.

He stalled a while, then that man with the scar on his chin walked in. Mr. Wompler was scared of him and hardly said anything. I could tell Mr. Wompler didn't like what was going on, but he left me with the man with the scar on his chin, whom he called Mr. McGuire. McGuire showed me a gun and said I better not try and get away. Then he took me downstairs and drove me here. We're in Brooklyn, aren't we?"

"Brooklyn," I said. "Go on."

"That's all I can tell you, Jason. They locked me in this room and went away. The window frame is nailed so you can't open the window, and see those bars? They're nailed right across the frame… You can't get out even if you smack the glass. They brought you in here, that Mr. McGuire and another man, and haven't been back since. Jason, what are they going to do with us?"

"I don't know," I admitted. Whatever it was, it wouldn't be good. I couldn't see the connection, though. Five O'Clock and Puggie were working for whoever had taken the Kincaid papers. They'd killed Jo-Anne, according to Guido, and they had sprayed him and me and Nostrand Avenue with bullets. But just how did they tie in with Wilson Wompler? Or my brother Ken, who was blackmailing himself?

"Jason, they're coming!" Steffy stiffened in my arms and we both turned to face the door. A key scraped in the lock. The door opened, then closed, admitting Puggie and a battered Five O'Clock to the room.

"He's up," Five O'Clock said. His left cheek was bruised and purple, his left eye swollen shut. His lips were swollen too. He seemed very sullen until he looked at me. Then he smiled. I must have looked even worse.

"I'm telling you," Puggie said, "it don't figure. We got no orders on this guy, so we can't just make him part of the package."

"The louse," said Five O'Clock. "He butted in, he goes along for the ride."

"We'll wait till we get told, see?"

Five O'Clock shrugged broad shoulders. "I ain't in no hurry," he said. "But I owe this guy something."

"That," said Puggie, "is your business."

"My pal," Five O'Clock said. "My buddy, Puggie. I done you favors."

"So what you want I should do?"

"Keep him covered. Keep the dame covered. I want to kick the teeth out of him."

Puggie nodded without expression and took a .45 automatic out from under his jacket. This close, it looked like an elephant gun. Five O'Clock said, "You sit still, lady. I ain't fooling."

Steffy looked at me. I nodded.

Five O'Clock grinned crookedly out of the unswollen side of his mouth. Then he hit me.

It was a pretty fair wallop and it spilled me over on my back. My bum shoulder started to ache again. "Get up," Five O'Clock said.

I climbed to hands and knees and got spilled again when Five O'clock's foot thudded against my ribs. Steffy screamed and Puggie told her to shut up.

"Get it over with," Puggie said.

"I ain't in no hurry," Five O'Clock reminded him and dug his heel into my back. I wasn't finished yet. I could have gotten to my feet before the count of ten and still made a fight of it. But there was Puggie and his .45, meant as much for Steffy as for me. I lay there and let Five O'Clock drag me up into a sitting position. Then he kicked me again and I was clawing at the worn threads of the carpet on the floor.

The hell with him, I thought. I'd come up fighting. I lay there a while, breathing dust from the carpet.

Five O'Clock returned with a water-soaked towel just as I climbed to hands and knees. He swung the towel like a flail and it almost tore my head off, but I stayed that way, on hands and knees. Steffy was sobbing.

"Holler, you bastard!" Five O'Clock screamed. "Why don't you holler?" He was swinging the towel again and while it had lost some of its moisture it was still wet and heavy. I rolled over on my good shoulder and plucked the towel from his hands, rolling again and scrambling to my feet. He came lumbering toward me, amazed that I could still operate after he'd done his worst. I slammed the wet towel across the side of his head, where it raised a red welt from ear to jaw as he fell.

"That's enough," Puggie said, waving his .45. "Drop that towel." It sounded ridiculous: drop that towel. I laughed and Steffy, who'd been crying, started to laugh, too. I dropped the wet towel on Five O'clock's face and he came up with it in his hands and mayhem in his eyes.

He screamed something meaningless, like one of II Duce's balcony speeches. It was easy to sidestep and shove him in the direction he was already traveling under a full head of steam. He plowed into the door and moaned and sat down there, mumbling to himself.

"You struck out," Puggie told him. "That's enough. Better stay put till the boss gets here."

"There are ways to kill a guy," Five O'Clock was promising himself, "and ways to kill a guy. Slow, so he dies an ounce at a time. That's how he's going to get it, Puggie. An ounce at a time."

"We better wait for the boss," repeated Puggie, lifting Five O'Clock to his feet and opening the door and ushering him outside.

We listened to the door being locked. We stood there looking at each other. Then I grinned. Steffy tried it too and said, "You look positively hideous. Jason, please hold me tight. You think they're going to kill us?"

"I don't know."

"But why?"

"I know too much. Still, I can't figure out why they brought you here."

"Jason, they can't…just…can they?"

I tried to comfort her. I cursed Puggie and Five O'Clock, and wondered who was behind them. Wompler? Was he man enough?

Suddenly we heard the door being unlocked again. It swung open. Someone was thrust into the room.

My brother Ken.

Chapter Seventeen

He immediately spun around and pounded on the door and twisted the knob futilely. He hadn't noticed us yet. "You can't do this to me," he said. "Let me out of here." It was all automatic. In such a situation, people say things like that. Ken was opening his mouth and the sounds were coming out, syllable following appropriate syllable. This was Ken, even when he faced death. Ken with his automatic, proper, socially acceptable responses.

Giving it up, he turned away from the door, meaning to inspect the room.

"Jason," he said abruptly, seeing us for the first time. "Maybe you can explain why they've brought me here, boy."

"Maybe you can tell me," I said.

"It's all so confusing." Ken limped toward us on his bad leg with the built-up heel and for the first time it was completely Ken's leg, Ken's injury, and not mine. He didn't notice my battered face at all, and that helped. "Pop Grujdzak called me," Ken said. "He wanted to know if Wilson Wompler was blackmailing me over his daughter. He seemed to know a lot about it. I told him the truth, how Julia had been unfaithful to me with Wompler and how Wompler was bleeding me dry because of it."

"That isn't the truth," I said. "You arranged for Wompler to blackmail you. You wanted it. You thought you could keep Julia in line that way. You thought if she figured Wompler had pictures—"

"What are you saying, Jason boy? What are you telling me? A man doesn't blackmail himself."

He was sick. Give him time and soon he wouldn't believe the truth himself. "Just go ahead with your story," I said.

"Pop Grujdzak told me he was calling from Wompler's and that his daughter was in bad trouble and it was my fault. I said how could that be, Julia was right with me. But it must have been you he meant, is that it, Stephanie?" This was the first word Ken had addressed to her. "What is it? Anything I can help you with?"

"Never mind Steffy," I said. "What happened next?"

"I rushed down to Wompler's because I had to get this blackmail business straightened out. Pop Grujdzak wasn't around any more. I was told he had gone to Brooklyn—after you."

"Who told you?"

"The policemen there with Wompler and that big blonde woman who works for him. Wompler was a broken man! You wouldn't recognize him if you saw him. Brace yourself, Jason boy. The cops said he'd confessed to murdering the Phyllis Kirk girl and stealing those Kincaid papers!"

I nodded grimly. At the beginning, it would have had to be Wompler, of course. He was the only one who knew about the papers. Phyllis Kirk had told him, and had died for it. But someone must have taken it from there.

Who?

Ken, who could have frightened Wompler out of the deal with a kind of reverse blackmail? *You're blackmailing me because I'm paying you to blackmail me, but try to get anyone to believe that.*

The girl Audrey, who must have known most of Wompler's secrets and could do more with them than he could?

Pop Grujdzak, maybe? He'd been on all sides of this thing right along. What was keeping him, anyway? Why wasn't he on hand, rescuing his daughter? In a police car, he didn't have to worry about speed limits or red lights.

Something was still chewing at the back of my mind.

Maybe it spelled Pop Grujdzak and maybe it didn't but right now there was no getting it out into the open where I could study it.

"Keep talking," I told Ken.

"Wompler said you had taken the blackmail pictures. Then the phone rang—it was for me. Somebody by the name of McGuire. Said he had the pictures at The House That Jack Built, and I should come out to get them."

"The cops at Wompler's place didn't question you? Ask you about that phone call?"

"Why should they?" Ken said. "I'm a reputable citizen. I wanted to lay my hands on the pictures as soon as possible, so I found a taxi and came over. I asked for McGuire, and he pulled a gun on me. Then he forced me in here, but I don't know why. Do you know what they want?"

It was almost funny. Ken had come streaking over the Williamsburg Bridge after me to maintain the fiction of blackmail. It wasn't necessary at all and he must have known that in the part of his mind which didn't do the motivating, yet he had come anyway. And might get killed for it.

The poor guy was really nuts!

But why had they sent for him? There was a connection between Ken's self-blackmail and the Kincaid business that I failed to see.

"Listen," I said, "did the police tell you your father-in-law was on his way here?"

"They certainly did. That's what I don't understand, Jason. Where is Pop Grujdzak?"

"A good question." I looked at Steffy.

"Don't stare at me like that. I can't answer for my father. Maybe he went to a Brooklyn precinct station first, I don't know." Steffy's voice trailed off lamely. With his own daughter in trouble, Pop Grujdzak wouldn't stop to get reinforcements, and Steffy knew it.

Whatever the reason, it looked like we'd have to do our own rescuing. I went to the window and tried it, but the frame and thick wooden cross-bars were nailed firmly. There was nothing in the room I could use to pry out the nails. I stood thinking, rubbing a circle of condensed moisture off the cold pane with the palm of my hand and staring at the snow still falling thick and white outside. The flakes fluttered and fell and formed an image for me of Jo-Anne smiling and saying she didn't care about anything as long as I wouldn't send her away.

And I wondered if Ken, Steffy and I would follow her and the others to oblivion, soon becoming nothing more than someone's fading memories.

I tried the door but its lock was as effective as the window nails. I found myself studying Ken's face, the sagging weakness where lips met jowls, the uncertain eyes. Somehow I felt sorry for him and all his frustrations and lackings and incompleteness. It was a new kind of sympathy, an objective sympathy. I didn't feel sorry for Ken for what I had done to him; I felt sorry for Ken because he was somehow gravely, tragically hollow. He had all the necessary assets. The arms and the legs and the features, the proper clothing. But he was not a physical man, not a mental man, not an emotional man. He was my brother Ken, the social man. He was all appearances.

"This is New York City," Ken said. "They can't do this to us. Not here, not now. This is a civilized place. There are police for such things. We have nothing to worry about."

My platitude of a brother.

Who sought respect and affection from people in general because he could never get close to people in particular.

My own platitudes were at least less negative. I'd go down fighting, I was thinking, the next time Five O'Clock or Puggie poked a head inside the door.

At that moment, they did. Both of them. And someone else. I stood there and stared and if my mouth wasn't on hinges my jaw would have joined my feet on the floor.

What was nagging at the back of my mind stopped nagging. I knew. I had fitted the pieces together, but too late.

Into the room, behind Five O'Clock and Puggie, walked Tad Barrett.

Chapter Eighteen

Ken said, "Mr. Barrett, you're a sight for sore eyes! Did you bring the police? Never mind what I agreed to pay you. I'm going to double it. That's right, double it. I was beginning to lose faith in you, but you certainly earned your money. Yes, sir."

"Shut up," Five O'Clock growled.

Barrett tugged a pipe out of the pocket of his snowy overcoat and filled the bowl from an oilskin pouch.

"It's one hell of a night for a ride," Puggie said, walking to the window and making it transparent with his sleeve.

"We'll wait. Maybe the snow will let up," Barrett said. I watched him puffing on his briar contentedly. I figured we had a reprieve as long as the pipe kept going, he was enjoying it so much.

"Who has the pictures?" Ken asked all of us. "I'll feel better after I burn them. Wait till my wife hears about this, she'll be delighted. Well, we all can make mistakes."

"Will someone shut him up?" Five O'Clock said.

My nose clogged again and I could no longer smell Barrett's pipe smoke. I said, "It had me all mixed up because it was Wompler first. Then it was you, Barrett. It was staring me right in the face all along, only I couldn't see it. I guess I'm a little too late."

"Too late," Barrett agreed.

"When Phyllis Kirk contacted Wompler about the Kincaid papers, he was interested all right. But not because he wanted to run an article in *Hush*. He figured my brother had taught him all there was to know about blackmail, and this was the real thing. This was big. With the income from this he could retire a rich man. Maybe he had Phyllis Kirk figured wrong, I don't know. My guess is that he saw her in her apartment and said they could split it down the middle blackmailing a few dozen of our most respected citizens. She was a scientist. She wasn't buying that. She'd merely thought with an article on the Kincaid stuff, a kind of preview mentioning no names, she could make herself a few bucks. She showed the papers only to prove she was on the inside, and how hot the possibilities were."

Barrett sat down on the bed and folded his arms, nibbling on his pipe stem and listening. Ken looked like he wanted to ask some questions, but Five O'Clock glared at him and he said nothing. Steffy was listening to my story in big-eyed silence. My horror story.

"So they had a difference of opinion. Probably Wompler overplayed his hand and maybe Phyllis Kirk tried to throw him out. But there were the Kincaid papers, worth a fortune in blackmail, enticing him. So he struggled, killed her accidentally or otherwise, and stole the papers. He was in business."

Barrett looked more interested. I began to hope my story might be worth another pipe load and wondered if Pop Grujdzak had lost his way in the Brooklyn streets and all that snow. I kept on talking.

"When I first went to visit Wompler he agreed to stop blackmailing Ken almost cheerfully, but he played it cagey about the Kincaid papers, denying everything. When he later changed his mind about blackmailing Ken, I should have realized my brother was…well, blackmailing himself."

"That," said Ken, "is incredible and you know it."

"Just shut up," I told him. "I didn't know you from a hole in the wall, Barrett, but like a fool I had to open up and tell you how I thought Wompler knew something about the Kincaid papers and probably had them in his possession. You see, that's what has been bothering me all the time! Wompler got all hot and bothered in Phyllis Kirk's apartment and killed her, but he wasn't big enough or tough enough for the other murders." I paused to wipe my nose with a flooded handkerchief. "You were the missing link, Barrett. The connection between Ken's blackmail and the Kincaid papers."

"You, hunting down blackmail, put me onto the papers. Sure," said Barrett. He must have known I was just stalling for time, filibustering until Pop Grujdzak could arrive. But he seemed interested. "So what?"

"So this. I laid the whole story in your lap. I even built up the papers and told you how important they were. I was worried about Jo-Anne and wanted you to know exactly what you were after.

That was my mistake—but it should have made me realize, later, that you'd taken over from Wompler!"

Barrett puffed and listened.

"Well, I don't know how you did it. Maybe you had enough on Wompler. Maybe you just strong-armed him, it doesn't matter. But you took it from there. I'd admitted to you that I didn't understand the code. Wompler didn't know that. You did, Barrett. So your boys tortured Jo-Anne for the code, then killed her to shut her mouth. You picked a spot that would throw suspicion on Wompler."

Barrett nodded. "You should have been a detective," he said.

"There's more. When Guido got a rumble on Five O'Clock and Puggie, he called you and left a message for me. He'd been able to learn they were the boys who'd worked on Jo-Anne for you, but the poor slob told you about it because that's what I'd said he should do. After that, it was easy. You got in touch with Puggie and Five O'Clock and they were waiting for us outside. And still I didn't get it!"

Neither Puggie nor Five O'Clock bothered to complain that I knew too much. Apparently my fate was no longer the subject of doubt or even polite conversation.

"While I was in the hospital," I went on, "Steffy here found out all she had to know about the pictures. She returned to Wompler's to get them after I left the hospital, and I was keeping you informed about it. What the hell, you were a private detective. You could help me. But I was so blind I didn't get it even after Audrey told me how Wompler had received a phone call, then made one.

"You called him, Barrett. You told him Steffy was on her way over. You let him know where he could reach Five O'Clock and Puggie, and while he probably didn't like it, he called them and had them come for Steffy. That didn't figure at first. Why should you care if Steffy collected the pictures? That had nothing to do with the Kincaid papers. But you had noticed she and I were getting pretty chummy. You were worried about what I might have told her...*Kerchoo!*"

"Sure," Barrett said. "You had enough information to figure out things, but you were too stupid. Not her. If you were blabbing to her like you were to me, she might guess the score. So I thought it best to bring her here with the rest of you."

"And get rid of all of us at once."

"That's right. Anyone who might lead the police to me."

"Ken—my brother—he didn't know about all this…"

"He knew about those pictures," Barrett said, not trying to justify himself, just explaining what a smart guy he was. "He was on a fake blackmail juggle with Wompler. If the cops started to lean on them, something might come up which could get the police interested enough to chase down that trail. That's why I have to get rid of this windbag—and his phony pictures too. Then nothing will remain to connect me with the Kincaid stuff. The police will never even know your brother hired me, or sent you to me. My name won't come up at all."

"You're forgetting Wompler."

"He doesn't know I'm in on this. Five O'Clock did all the dirty work, and I'm paying him for it."

I let go a couple of sneezes.

"Bless you," Steffy said.

I had to keep on stalling. Where the hell was her father? "Barrett," I said, "Wompler could still shoot off his mouth about those pictures. And probably he's wise to the fact that Ken hired you about the photos—"

"You let me worry about Wompler."

"And Audrey. Don't forget the lady wrestler."

"And Audrey. And anyone else I have to worry about. One thing at a time, Chase."

I didn't mention Aunt Emma.

However, I still had one good stall. He would have to listen to this.

I managed to get off a fine burst of laughter, as if something had occurred to me that was highly amusing. The effect was somewhat spoiled by another vigorous sneeze, but I hastened to say, "You think you're smart, Barrett. Yet actually you've bungled badly."

"That so?"

"Wompler may not know you have him pegged for his part in Ken's blackmail act—probably he doesn't know, or you'd be more worried about the possibility of his talking. Unless he had something against you, he would have no reason to mention that phony shakedown—which would only make himself look even worse in the eyes of police, D.A., and jury." I forced another laugh. "But you've forgotten one thing he is sure to mention."

"What's that?" Barrett waited tensely.

"You sent an operative to Wompler's apartment. Both Wompler and Audrey can say a Barrett agency man was the last person seen with Jo-Anne while she was still alive."

Barrett's tenseness stayed with him, but only for another moment or two. Then suddenly he was smiling, smiling in a superior, self-satisfied way.

I realized in that instant why he had let me go on talking. He had been listening to me go over the whole affair, especially his part in it, just to check on whether he had forgotten anything— whether I might not be aware of some flaw in his scheme which he had overlooked.

And it seems I had come up with such a flaw. Which was why he was wearing that self-satisfied smirk. His game with me had succeeded. Now he was forewarned, and changed plans accordingly.

"All right, then my name *will* come up with the police," he said, thinking aloud. "The police will know from *me* that I had a man pick up Jo-Anne. I'll volunteer that information—whether or not Wompler has already told them. I'll produce the man, too. He'll say merely that he started to bring her to me—but she broke away from him and fled. After all, he had no power to arrest her."

"But why was he on her tail at all?"

"Just what the cops will ask," said Barrett. "My explanation will be legitimate. You had hired me to find the missing papers— maybe locate the missing Jo-Anne in the process. My first step, in view of what you had told me about Wompler, logically was to send a man to his place. And there the man bumped into Jo-Anne—"

"The hell with you," I said, remembering her.

Puggie had cleared the window pane and was busy looking outside. "Still snowing," he said. "Hell of a night for a ride."

"The snow will keep people in, including cops," Barrett told him. "We'll have the street to ourselves, so it won't be so bad. Anyway, we'd better not wait any more. Get the car, boys."

Five O'Clock nodded happily and went to the door. I wondered how long it would be before he got back. Maybe Pop was outside, I thought. Maybe he had the place staked out with all the law in

Brooklyn and was just waiting for someone to poke a head out of the door.

"Let's wrap this all up," Barrett said. "I'd like the pictures, Chase."

I made a production of going through my pockets. I still hadn't given up entirely on Pop Grujdzak, but if he was lost, he was good and lost. Pop could have been here twice already. I looked at Steffy, who sighed and squeezed my hand. I took the envelope of pictures from the inside pocket of my jacket and handed it to Barrett.

He opened the flap and withdrew the pictures, studying them. "This all of it?" he said, and choked on the last word as Ken lumbered across the room, huge and ungainly, to grasp and claw at him with awkward ineffectiveness.

"You give me those! Let me have those pictures!"

Barrett slapped him on the jaw. Ken rained blows on Barrett's shoulders and chest with soft fists, clumsy slow-motion blows.

"Ken," I said. "He's going to destroy them. He's going to do what you want anyhow, Ken. Cut it out."

Ken blubbered. Barrett was catching the soft blows on his open hands now, smiling.

"Hey!" Barrett suddenly roared. One of Ken's fists had cuffed the bridge of his nose, bringing tears to his eyes. Puggie went rushing across the room. At first, I was going to stop him. But I needed my strength for whatever was to come. My shoulder was throbbing and numb. I was sneezing and sniffling. I stood by and watched Puggie yank at Ken's arm and spin him around, then bury his left fist in Ken's soft midsection. Ken leaned over slowly and covered his belly with clasped hands, bowing. The air had made a noise rushing from his lungs and out his mouth, which still hung open and formed a big O. He staggered three steps toward me, still clasping his hands over his belly, then fell heavily. My own brother, but I didn't try to catch him.

While I was watching Ken trying to suck air back into his lungs, Five O'Clock returned.

"Man, I ain't never seen such snow," he said.

"The car has chains?" Barrett wanted to know.

"Snow tires."

I sneezed. Steffy had gone into the bathroom and returned with a glass of water for Ken, but Puggie took it from her hands and sloshed the contents in Ken's face.

"I can't...move...at...all," Ken gasped.

"Why'd you have to hit him so hard?" Barrett said.

"He didn't look so soft," Puggie answered.

They got more water for Ken and let him drink it this time, but he gagged on it. They slapped his face gently, then not so gently, Puggie on one side and Five O'Clock on the other, while Barrett burned the pictures of Steffy and Wompler. They stood him up and walked him back and forth, the soft, hard-looking hugeness of him sagging between them.

"You okay now?" Puggie asked.

"I'm going to throw up. I'll feel much better if you let me throw up."

"Hell with that. Choke on it," Five O'Clock said. "You can walk." Five O'Clock opened the door for us and demonstrated how his .45 could point at us through the cloth of his coat. Barrett was too smart to pack a gun, but Puggie had one too. All we had, Steffy and me and Ken, were fading hopes. Where was Pop Grujdzak?

Barrett went out first into the hallway, followed by Ken and Steffy, then Puggie, then me. Five O'Clock brought up the rear with his cannon. We trooped down the stairs that way. Auntie didn't even look up from her magazine when we passed her desk.

You read about those things, how they take you through a crowded bar or something with a gun in your back and no one is wise. I was hoping we'd get the chance to prove truth might be stranger than fiction but less improbable. Hell, I'd attract someone's attention. I'd make it known we were prisoners. I'd trip a guy or spill his drink or anything. Let them try and shoot at us in a crowded bar like that.

Downstairs, The House That Jack Built was empty.

It smelled of beer and smoke and always would, but there was no one around and the only light in the place was the red, yellow and blue glow from the juke box. We marched by the juke box and along the bar and out through the front door, which did not even tinkle behind us. Mr. Jack must have been Puggie's brother or Five O'clock's. The snap lock snicked shut behind us.

We sank to our ankles in the soft snow, which was still falling feather-light and silent. Five O'Clock got behind the wheel of a black four-door Chrysler, three or four years old, waiting at the curb. Barrett told Steffy to climb in beside him, then rounded out the front-seat contingent himself. Ken and I sat in back with Puggie between us holding the .45 on his lap. Puggie leaned over and pressed the little lock studs on my side and Ken's.

Then Five O'Clock started the car.

I couldn't see Pop Grujdzak anywhere. Or any other cops.

Nostrand Avenue was deserted.

There were only the six of us, and the sound the tires made singing across the snow.

Chapter Nineteen

Five O'Clock drove the Chrysler with consummate caution, taking his foot off the gas and slowing the big car to a crawl whenever we had to turn on the soft, trackless snow. Up front, you could hear the defroster purring faintly to keep the windshield from fogging over.

I asked, and got, permission to reach for my handkerchief and blow my nose.

"It's like the old days, ain't it?" Five O'Clock called over his shoulder to Puggie.

"Just look where you're driving," Barrett said, puffing smoke.

"What I mean," Five O'Clock went right on talking, "you steal a car and a license plate from some other car and rent a garage for a drop, leaving the car there till you need it. You wait and get to hoping it'll be soon, the ride. Then, before you know, you're ready. With a three-part package. Man."

"You sure the Park is best?" Puggie leaned forward and asked his partner.

"Search me. Prospeck Park, that's what the boss says."

With them, this was a livelihood. Nothing slipshod about the way they performed their duties. There was obedience and skill and planning. There was care and timing and a deadly lack of emotional involvement. Things had been slow since their youth, when Murder, Inc., had folded its Brooklyn tent and barnstormed all over the country. But now, thanks to Barrett, they were in business again.

"Prospect Park it is," Barrett said.

"In the old days they used to hide packages down in Flatlands," Puggie told him. He wasn't complaining, but offering an item of information.

"It's built up since then, Puggie. Plenty of houses and people."

"Yeah, but you could hide the bodies out in the Flatlands dumps."

"Here, the bodies will be found," said Barrett. "But we won't be."

It was us they were talking about, with the objectivity of businessmen completing a routine transaction. In Barrett there wasn't even the hint of remorse or conscience. Some folks, they say, are born incapable of those things. Often they behave beyond suspicion, those sick people, until it's too late. Sometimes they're good-looking, charming, intelligent. Maybe they liked to pull the wings off flies more than other kids. But boys will be boys. If they served in the Army they made lousy soldiers, complaining and griping all the time about discipline, until they got a taste of combat. They often won medals, then, and were afraid but didn't go stiff and inadequate with fear like some of their buddies. They felt above the crowd. They were arrogant. Laws didn't apply to them. They could kill you with an absolute lack of concern if it suited them. They were called psychopathic personalities, P.P.'s, and Barrett was one of them.

It looked as if we were going to die.

Nameless Brooklyn streets slipped by, white-mantled and silent. Five O'Clock seemed to know the neighborhood, braking for his turns automatically even though you could hardly see through the clouds of snow swirling at the windshield.

The car was long and black. A hearse.

We were riding to our own funeral in our own hearse and I thought I could probably open the door on my side and dive out into the snow, risking a broken bone, and get away. But there was Ken on the other side of Puggie, and Steffy sitting between Five O'Clock and Barrett.

We passed through a residential neighborhood with snow-roofed houses and big, bare, snowy trees all looking alike. A man in a fur-collared storm coat was walking a dog, a spotted terrier that rolled and frolicked in the snow as we went by.

"It ain't a fit night out for a dog, even. That's cruelty to animals," said Five O'Clock, guffawing.

"Watch your driving," Barrett told him. His pipe had gone out.

I sneezed. The residential neighborhood faded into a business area, all the store windows and neon tubing dark. There was a subway kiosk on our left, lettered with the words Interboro Rapid Transit. In the morning it would swallow the hundreds of sleepy-eyed strap-hangers staring at the tabloid headlines which might say, if the late editions hadn't gone to press yet, *TRIPLE MUR-DER IN PROSPECT PARK. The bodies of two men, identified as Kenneth and Jason Chase, brothers, and Stephanie Grujdzak, the attractive daughter of a Manhattan Homicide police lieutenant, were found early this morning in Prospect Park.*

"We're almost there," Puggie said.

I sneezed and took a deep breath through my mouth and thought of all the things the strap-hangers would think and leaned forward before Puggie had time to stop me, over Five O'clock's shoulder, wrenching the steering wheel hard to the left. Puggie cursed and I was hoping Five O'Clock would jam on the brakes instinctively and send the big Chrysler into a skid. I couldn't tell because I was fighting with Puggie for the .45 which he was trying to bring around to kill me right here instead of in the Park.

It was like an atomic explosion heard from the general vicinity of ground zero when the .45 went off in the closed car, blowing a hole in the roof. Puggie's mouth was working as if he were still cursing, but I couldn't hear a thing.

The Chrysler had skidded across the snow to the curb on the left side of the street, where the engine stalled. Puggie had netted only powder burns on his face and in his eyes for firing the .45. He sat there in pain, staring at the gun, and I figured he wouldn't get around to using it for a while.

I yanked the door open on my side and plunged into the snow. There was another shot sooner than I had expected, but Ken had deflected Puggie's arm. I whirled and got Five O'Clock's door open from the outside, while he sat there grinding the starter and trying to kick the car over. He was groping inside his coat for a gun when I tugged him out into the snow by his lapels and stepped on his face there in the snow and yelled, "Get the hell out, Steffy!"

She came sliding across the seat while Barrett was trying to hold her there. He wound up with her coat only and she'd be cold but maybe alive.

"You dirty—" Puggie howled, and stuck his face out into the snow. I hit him before he could fire the .45 again, but he kept on coming. When he got all the way outside there was room for Ken to follow. I looked at him once to make sure he was on his feet. Then I grabbed Steffy's hand and started running across the snow.

Puggie's .45 or Five O'clock's or both exploded four times behind us. I turned and saw Ken falling forward in the bright snow-reflected glare of a street light. A .45 slug had entered his skull from behind and ripped his face open in front. He fell like that, with no face left, sprawling across the snow.

"The subway," I told Steffy. "We've got to reach that subway."

We kept running. Later I could think of Ken and what they had done to him, but now I was lifting my feet and setting them down in the snow and lifting them again and holding Steffy's hand as we ran, and feeling feverish. We'd put some distance between us and Five O'Clock, who was leading Puggie and Barrett across the snow behind us, but they were still too close. Their .45's roared, slugs caroming off the brick taxpayer wall beside us and peppering our faces with chips of brick and mortar.

We reached the kiosk, where Steffy tripped on the slippery top step. I righted her and plunged down into the musty dampness of the subway with her. We slammed through the exit gate and onto the platform; the station agent must have been too sleepy to notice us.

"A train," Steffy said. "Pray for a train."

We ran along the platform, which was littered with newspapers and gum wrappers, but deserted. Barrett and his hoods came plunging down the stairs behind us, but we could hear the rumble of a train approaching.

I grinned wildly at Steffy and was about to tell her how we could get off the train a few stations further down the line and contact the police in perfect safety. The train flashed by, roaring and spitting angry blue sparks at the tracks. The center tracks, far from the platform. It was an express and kept on going and you could catch a quick glimpse of the sleepy faces in the windows, framed by yellow light.

"Jason!" Steffy cried. "Oh, God, Jason."

I took her hand again and kept running along the platform. Five O'Clock or Puggie fired again and the explosion echoed in the tunnel. The station agent yelled something.

A sign said there was an exit to the street at the other end of the long platform, in the direction from which the express train had come. We'd make it, I thought. They couldn't shoot accurately at this distance in the dimness of the subway tunnel.

We'd make it.

But a gate barred the exit at the end of the platform, a sign informing us that it was an auxiliary exit open only during rush hours. Five O'Clock came tearing down the platform, not fifty paces away, with Puggie and Barrett right behind him. Even if a train came now, it would be too late.

"Jump!" I told Steffy, and leaped off the platform myself. I waited for her on the tracks and caught her as she came down. Five O'Clock snapped a shot off and the slug splintered the third-rail guard. Then we were running along the tracks and left the station behind us, plunging into the darkness of the tunnel. Every few yards or so a dirty naked bulb cast dim shadows that lost themselves quickly in the gloom. There was a three-foot space between the tracks and the wall, where occasional safety niches had been hewn in the cement. Here away from the station the third rail was unprotected and looked innocent but could electrocute a man.

We ran and heard them pounding along the tracks behind us. Steffy's foot caught on the ties and she screamed as she fell forward, flat between the tracks. I helped her to her feet, but she was scowling and sobbing with pain and said, "My ankle. It's my ankle."

I carried her to the darkness of one of the safety niches, a foot-deep depression in the cement wall, the size of a doorway. We flattened ourselves there and waited. Five O'Clock came first, so close I could have reached out and touched him. He stared straight ahead, his .45 ready. Barrett was a dozen yards behind him, with Puggie trailing.

"Hold it," Barrett said, panting. "I don't hear them." The three of them stopped, with Puggie directly opposite our niche.

"They're hiding somewhere."

"I can't see nothing," Five O'Clock said.

My stuffed nose started to itch and tickle on the inside. The muscles gathered themselves for a sneeze. Steffy looked at me and saw my face contorting and her lips formed the words, "Ob, no." If it wasn't so tragic it would have been funny. It suddenly was the most important thing in the world to keep from sneezing. I thought of the only remedy ever devised. I held a finger under my nose.

It didn't work.

I sneezed and in my ears it sounded louder than the express train which had roared by. At the same moment I leaped from the niche and was grappling with Puggie before he had the time to use his .45. It was between us as we fought back and forth across the tracks. Puggie was trying to force me against the raised third rail. If he succeeded, I thought, he'd fry not only me but himself as well, and die with a surprised look on his face.

Five O'Clock and Barrett came running back through the tunnel toward us, just as Puggie got a leg behind me and pushed me over it. I went down hard but twisted away from the rail, then saw the muzzle blast as Five O'Clock fired on the run. Puggie clutched his side and tumbled down after me. I rolled aside and you could smell it, the clothing and the flesh sizzling. I picked up Puggie's .45 and shot Five O'Clock in the chest as he lumbered toward me.

I pulled the trigger again, but the automatic clicked on an empty chamber. I hurled it at Barrett and got to my feet.

There was the faint drip, drip of water somewhere as snow melted and leaked through a crack in the roof of the tunnel. There was the sound of Barrett's hard breathing as we grappled there on the tracks and occasionally you could hear Steffy sobbing. There was something else.

A distant rumbling sound which grew louder. A pulsing blue glow far down the tunnel.

Local train rumbling toward the station on this track!

Barrett butted me with his head and got hold of my ears and tried it again. I think I bit his scalp but then he doubled me over, slicing the edge of his palm across my kidney. His knee came up against my chest, spilling me on my back near where Five O'Clock lay. Writhing clear as Barrett leaped at me, feet first, I jumped up. My left arm dangled at my side now. It had weight but no strength. There was a roaring in my ears, engulfing me.

The train took shape down the track. You could see it now, filling the tunnel and growing larger every second.

I ducked under Barrett's wild swing and caught him with a rabbit punch as he went by. He turned and I hit him again, but now the train was filling the world with noise and light and its enormous bulk. I dove for the niche in the wall and pressed myself flat there with Steffy.

The train roared up and past us and Barrett screamed briefly.

* * * *

There were cops and white-uniformed doctors and crowds of reporters and flashbulbs. There were questions. There was cooperation between Pop Grujdzak and the Brooklyn Homicide boys, and cooperation with the District Attorney's office. There was a lack of sleep and bleary eyes and a lot of shouting while the whole thing came out.

There was Julia who would not know happiness for a long time and might never know it again. And Pop Grujdzak saying it was all right, everything was all right, she could come home with him and Emma.

And there was Steffy who kept on kissing me and didn't seem to mind that she'd catch my cold…

Seems Pop Grujdzak's car had had a flat on the bridge, which had slowed him up. So he'd put out an S.O.S. for prowl cars to hunt us down. Only trouble was, he sent them to Livonia Street, Five O'clock's only stamping ground that the cops knew about. They had raided a numbers set-up there only the day before, but now they all tore Livonia apart again before getting a lead that sent them to The House That Jack Built, then through the Park after us.

"We found the missing Kincaid papers in that joint," Pop said. "Also, a lot of girls."

"I won't tell Aunt Emma on you," I promised.

He actually tried to smile.

Old Pop with his rasping voice. It would be different from now on, he kept telling me. I'd saved his daughter's life.

Different or the same, I didn't care. I just wanted a few gallons of hot brandy and a lot of blankets.

And either way I was going to marry his daughter.

www.ingramcontent.com/pod-product-compliance
Lightning Source LLC
Chambersburg PA
CBHW020249150626
46552CB00020B/734